Look out for James Harris's next book,

coming soon!

THE UNBELIEVABLE BISCUIT FACTORY

(100% definitely not a
SUPER-SECRET SCIENCE LAB
filled with
orange fluffy
monsters)

JAMES HARRIS

Illustrated by Loretta Schauer

HODDER CHILDREN'S BOOKS

First published in Great Britain in 2021 by Hodder and Stoughton

1 3 5 7 9 10 8 6 4 2

A CIP catalogue record for this book
is available from the British Library.

ISBN 978 1 444 95559 0

Typeset in Museo Slab by Couper Street Type Co.
Printed and bound in Great Britain by Clays Ltd. Elcograf S.p.A

The paper and board used in this book
are made from wood from responsible sources.
Hodder Children's Books

An imprint of
Hachette Children's Group
Part of Hodder and Stoughton
Carmelite House
50 Victoria Embankment
London EC4Y 0DZ

An Hachette UK Company
www.hachette.co.uk

www.hachettechildrens.co.uk

For Mum

Chapter 1

WOOOOOOO

Normalton

Normalton is a small town in the middle of England. It is known for being totally normal. It is so normal that the concept of 'normal' was named after Normalton, and not the other way round. Normalton is the site of the Biscuit Factory, which is a totally normal biscuit factory that makes totally normal biscuits like a totally normal biscuit factory would do. It is absolutely, 100% *not* a Super-Secret Science Lab in disguise. Look, we wouldn't have called it 'the Biscuit Factory' if it wasn't a totally normal factory that made totally normal biscuits, would we?

[extracted from *Biccypedia*]

There was a big rabbit in the front garden. I say 'big' because it looked big, but that might have been an illusion caused by the massive platform boots it was wearing. They were bright red and shiny, and the heels were yellow and quite built-up, so really it was difficult to properly tell how big it was. It was definitely a rabbit, though, with its furry face and ridiculous taste in footwear. No human would wear boots like that, I thought, as I rubbed the sleep out of my eyes, readying myself for a properly *motto* Saturday.

Because it was Saturday morning, I could hear the *thumpa thumpa thumpa* 'ugh, ow, OH HECKHECKHECKAAA!' of my mum doing her exercise DVD downstairs. And on top of all that there was the shrill, piercing *WOOOOOOO* of the old air-raid siren on top of Carpenter's Hill, which indicated the Biscuit Factory was having some kind of crisis or other. If I'd had to guess, which I didn't, but sometimes guessing can be fun, I would have guessed that today's Biscuit Factory emergency was rabbit-based.

2

I launched into my morning routine. I don't need to go into huge detail about the routine. You probably have one yourself. I did some water-based sprucing up and got dressed super-quick. And then I reached for my hairbrush.

The bulk of my routine is taken up with hair admin. I have naturally frizzy hair, so I have a heck of a job getting my hair to behave. As I battered my hair with a hairbrush shaped like half a unicorn (it had broken two days ago due to my hair being so unruly), I wandered back to my window. The rabbit was still out there, crouching behind a patch of rhubarb. I idly wondered what it was hiding from, and where it had got those boots. I know I shouldn't have been wondering about the rabbit, or its choice of footwear, because it's not allowed, but I couldn't help it. And then a big black van with 'See Nothing! Say Nothing! Sorted!' written on its side screeched into our street and five Biscuitrons jumped out.

The Biscuitrons work for the Biscuit Factory.

We are not really supposed to talk about the Biscuitrons. We are supposed to ignore them if we see them. In fact, we're not really even allowed to see them, even if we do see them, which we do (or don't), a lot (i.e. never, of course). The same goes for things like big rabbits standing up on two legs.

The Biscuitrons were dressed head-to-toe in light brown overalls, the colour of custard creams. They marched into our front garden and circled the rabbit, as I tugged at a madly disobedient clump of hair.

Then the rabbit got bigger. Or at least it stood up straighter and lifted up its front paws. It looked like it was going to surrender. I didn't see what happened next because one of the Biscuitrons turned and looked up at me. He mimed closing curtains. It was an awkward moment because if I wasn't supposed to be looking at him, how was I supposed to know he wanted me to stop looking at him? It was a puzzle that didn't seem to bother him, because he did another curtain-closing mime, so I closed the curtains and kept brushing.

Hair tamed, or at least more or less obeying gravity, and all other aspects of my routine completed successfully, I went down for breakfast.

'Heck,' said Mum, every tendon and muscle straining as she attempted to copy what the muscly man on her laptop screen was doing. 'Heck heck heck. Morning, Haddie. Heck.'

She called me Haddie because that is my name. Sometimes I am called Hadz because that is my name, too. Sometimes I am called H-bomb. Actually, I am never called H-bomb but gosh I'd like to be.

'Smoothie?' I asked.

'Rrrrrr, heck!' she said, so I made us both a kale, blueberry and banana puddle. Apparently if you eat food in gloopy liquid form, with miscellaneous bits bobbing about in it, it's super-good for you and you will live for ever. That's what my mum seems to think, although why she would want to live for ever when every day seems to be so full of pain, I couldn't tell you. Today she was exercising so hard it looked like her whole body was crying. Armpit tears were flying all over the kitchen.

'Oh heck, that feels good,' said Mum, against all the evidence, as the man on the screen told her she was the very best version of herself she could possibly be. I thought that was unlikely but I said nothing as I handed her the smoothie.

'Siren's going,' she said.

'Uh-huh,' I agreed. I didn't mention the rabbitty commotion in the garden because in Normalton we don't talk about that kind of thing.

'You should probably stay in today, do you think?'

'Oh heck, Mum! Band practice!'

'Haddie! What have I told you about language?'

**YOU HAVE 1 NEW NOTIFICATION:
A MESSAGE ABOUT LANGUAGE**

As you have probably noticed, when people get vexed they sometimes use words that they absolutely shouldn't use. In this story, things get vexatious pretty quickly, and they stay vexatious until about five pages from the end, and all the characters have lots to say about the vexations they face, so I have decided to install a language filter on this book. Every time someone (especially an old person) says a word I'm not allowed to say, like 'heck', or 'heck,' or even 'heck', it will come out in this book as 'heck'. Heck, it's working already!

'You've told me all kinds of things about language,' I said. She has. She's an English teacher, so I hear a lot about language every day. She's also a single mum who does ridiculous exercise routines every morning, so I hear a lot of interesting language that I'm not allowed to use. My mum is complicated and no mistake. If my mum was a recipe you'd need to go to five different shops just to get the ingredients.

'Well then,' she said.

There was no arguing with that, because what did it even mean?

And then the siren stopped.

'Sounds like the emergency's over,' I said. 'So . . . band practice?'

'Are you sure you wouldn't rather stay in with me? I've got a new aromatherapy diffuser,' said Mum.

'Wow. Um . . .' I didn't really know what to say about that. Mum doesn't like going out, which is fine, but my feeling is that if I go out and do stuff, and then come back and tell her about all the stuff that I've done, then maybe next time she'll want to come out and do stuff, too.

Mum is a bit weird. She buys too many candles that make the house smell of 'calm' or 'contemplation' or 'cookie dough', and she eats too much broccoli, which makes the house smell of something else altogether.

So yeah, a bit weird.

But when you think about it, it's all kinds of weird out there, in the world. But in here, at home, it's our kind of weird and that's comforting.

Anyway, at that precise moment I didn't realise exactly how weird things were going to get out there.

Maybe if I had known, I might have stayed inside with Mum and her new aromatherapy diffuser and her veggie toots and her comforting kind of weirdness.

But if I had, the world would have ended.

I'll leave it to you to decide whether I made the right decision.

'I'll see you later, Mum,' I said. And then I went out and saved the world.

Chapter 2

RAAAR!

Biccypedia

Biccypedia is the in-house online encyclopedia of the Biscuit Factory. It can only be accessed by Biscuit Factory operatives. It is called 'Biccypedia' because we like a laugh at the Biscuit Factory. We're always saying things like, 'Oh crumbs!' or 'That's the way the cookie crumbles!' although we never say things like, 'Oh no, a big monster just crawled out of this hole in reality we've opened! That's not very Nice' because a) we don't open holes in reality and b) the 'nice' in 'Nice biscuits' isn't pronounced 'nice', it's pronounced 'nice', which means the joke doesn't work.

[extracted from *Biccypedia*]

I stepped out of my house and . . .

Oh, just so we're clear, I'm not going to save the world in this chapter. Actually, I don't save the world until quite near the end of the book, because that's traditional for books. You don't save the world in chapter two and then spend 27 chapters going on about how everything's all rainbows and cupcakes and unicorns now it's been saved. You spend 27 chapters writing about things getting worse and worse and worse, and *then* you save the world. And I hereby promise there are no rainbows, cupcakes or unicorns in this book, apart from the half a unicorn in chapter one.

Also, I didn't really even *mean* to save the world, I just wanted to play my guitar with my friends.

Now all that is clear, I think we can get on with the story.

So, I stepped out of the house. There was a pile of Biscuitrons on our front lawn, all bruised and battered. There was no sign of the rabbit.

'. . . Ohhh heck . . .' one of the Biscuitrons said quietly in a tone that suggested regret and poor life choices, but I just ignored him and kept walking because I wasn't supposed to be looking at them and anyway I had other things to think about, because today we were going to have a band practice.

Yes! I *am* in a band, thank you for asking. We're really good but we'll never be famous because we're better than that.

On that particular day we were called Raaar! which I know is a terrible name but names are hard and we'd had lots of them. Fidget Winners, Bacon Wendyhouse, UMWELT!, Twin Poops, Heckington, Bazookalele, Womble Death Trap. I could go on.

I play guitar and sing. I am truly fabooly at it apart from one problem: all the chords.

When I decided we would be in a band I bought a book with all the chords in and honestly I just could not get my fingers round even the easiest ones on page one.

I tried for ages, at least until lunchtime, but it became clear my stupid fingers WILL NOT STRETCH THAT WAY. So I decided to make up my own chords. Because who says the person who wrote that chord book found all the chords?

So our songs are full of chords like C bomb maboomboom, G willikers, A major catastrophe, E splat manga, etc. etc.

It is hard to describe what these chords sound like but if you imagine our music is Godzilla, and your ears are Tokyo . . . why, that's the great sound of Raaar!

The band is me, playing guitar and sort-of singing, and Naomi who plays bass, and George who swears he'll get a drum kit for Christmas, and who would lie about a thing like that?

I went to call for George. George's house was a lot like mine, only it didn't currently have a pile of battered Biscuitrons on the front lawn. I rang the doorbell and Mrs George opened the door.

'Have you seen his little smile!' she said, right at my face. She was laughing. 'He's so useful! I love him!'

'Morning, Mrs George. He is useful, isn't he?' I said. George *was* super-useful. Drummers are very hard to find.

'Would you like to push him around the carpet for a bit?' said Mrs George.

'I . . . I don't think so,' I said. 'I think we'll just go to band practice if that's OK.'

'He really does suck up all the dirt,' said Mrs George. 'And he never stops smiling! Hilarious!'

My mum is weird but George's family are really weird. Even though I had just now realised George's mum wasn't talking about George at this point, she was talking about the Vinny Vacuum cleaner that was in the hall behind her, a squat, bright blue cylinder of a thing with a smiley face painted on the front of it.

But who gets all loved-up about a vacuum cleaner? I ask you! She said it was hilarious. It's not hilarious, it's literally a big bag of choredom boredom with a face drawn on it. Old people are bonkers, and they lie to themselves all the time. Oh yes, hoovering will be a right old chuckle with Vinny Vacuum. LOOK AT HIS SMILEY FACE! As I lug him around from room to room doing housework. As if.

'I'm here for George,' I said.

'Oh, him,' said Mrs George. 'George!'

'Hey up,' said George, pattering down the stairs behind his mum. He wasn't smiling. He had a worried look on his face but that's how his face always is. He was carrying his 'drum kit' – three Tupperware boxes, a biscuit tin and an old maraca.

His mum looked at him, then at the Vinny Vacuum, and sighed. 'If you can't be useful, you could at least smile,' she said.

'OK, Mum, sorry, Mum,' said George, and off we went, heading for the Community Centre.

Along the way we caught up with Naomi carrying her bass guitar. She always just sort of turns up like that. I've never been to Naomi's house. I don't know where she lives. She is a mystery, wrapped in an enigma, wrapped in extremely cool clothes.

'Hi, Naomi,' I said.

Naomi said nothing, she just nodded in a way that made her amazing hair move really amazingly. She is so cool.

As we walked, I talked about how exciting band practice was going to be because of the new song I had written and also the new chord I had invented.

'That's the best news ever,' said George and Naomi in unison, clapping their hands and dancing.

I mean, I expect that's what they said. I was busy organising our schedules in my head, what songs we'd play, when to break for snackage, etc. etc. – basically all the stuff that you have to think about when you are a creative genius who does everything in the band.

George and Naomi don't write songs. That's probably for the best because if you have someone in your band as truly fabooly at writing songs and inventing new chords as I was then it would probably be pointless for anybody else to even try. That's what I thought, anyway, and George and Naomi totally agreed with me.

The new chord I had invented that morning was called F minus and it was going to sound like nothing else on Earth. I couldn't wait to play it for them. We kept walking.

'Um. So, Haddie? I think I have an idea for a song,' said George.

'Yes, you do!' I agreed. 'I just told you what it is – it's got F minus in it!'

'No, I mean . . .' said George, and he might have said some other stuff – he often did – but I was too excited about F minus to listen to him. And then we were at the Community Centre.

Chapter 3

SKA-DANNNNNG

Anomalies

Anomalies are things that should not be where they are, or, alternatively, things that are not where they should be. If you see a thing that shouldn't be where it is, or, alternatively, if you DON'T see a thing that isn't where it should be, and you think this might be an anomaly, please note that ANOMALIES DO NOT HAPPEN AT THE BISCUIT FACTORY because we just make biscuits, don't we, so you either *didn't* see the thing that *was* where it should be, or you *did* see the thing that *wasn't* where it should be. We hope that's clear.

[extracted from *Biccypedia*]

I love the Community Centre. It has toilets and plug sockets and Wi-Fi and a vending machine that sells pickled-onion-flavoured things. You could live there quite happily.

We practically do live there. We try to practise as often as possible because if you want to make a truly awesome noise you have to practise. Sometimes people will walk past the hut and shout, 'What the heck's that noise?' and we will shout back, 'It's exactly the noise we want it to be, you plum!' only we won't say 'you plum' because that's rude but we will be thinking it.

As George and Naomi set up their gear, I walked over to the storage space at the back and opened the cupboard doors in slow motion. Golden light bathed the room, red smoke billowed forth, and the sound of a billion angels singing **'WOAH YEAH!'** rang out as I reached in and grasped the neck of *El Jirafa Tremendo*.

Which is to say, 'I got my guitar out of the cupboard.' The light and the dry ice etc. might not have actually happened but this is my book and I thought occasionally adding a few special effects and a soundtrack might make things more exciting for you.

WOAH YEAH!

El Jirafa Tremendo is my guitar. Mum makes me keep El Jirafa Tremendo and my amplifier in the Community Centre for the same reason you don't keep a tiger in the bathroom cupboard: El Jirafa Tremendo is dangerous. I mean, Mum *says* it's because El Jirafa Tremendo is 'irritating' and was 'making life very difficult and sad', but she *means* that it is 'dangerous'.

In case you are wondering, I call my guitar 'El Jirafa Tremendo' because El Jirafa Tremendo is her name.

YOU HAVE 1 NEW NOTIFICATION:
A MESSAGE ABOUT EL JIRAFA TREMENDO

The story of how El Jirafa Tremendo and I met is shrouded in mystery. Some say she was bequeathed to me by a friendly wizard.

Some say I pulled her from deep within a rock on an ancient plain. Others say she was a gift from the gods of Olympus or Asgard or Glastonbury. Still others suggest I won her in a high stakes game of conkers with the Devil herself. None of those stories is completely true.

However El Jirafa Tremendo and I truly met, whether it was on the outer rim of a distant groovy galaxy or the budget musical instruments section of a popular retail website, El Jirafa Tremendo is very important to me. If I didn't have a guitar, I would just be a girl that nobody took any notice of. With El Jirafa Tremendo I am a girl with a guitar that nobody takes any notice of. But my goodness they have to work really hard to ignore me, because I am LOUD.

'Ouch!'

George, having sat himself down and arranged his Tupperware boxes around him, had tried to twirl a drumstick between his fingers and poked himself in the eye. He is basically a long series of accidents waiting to happen. If he's lucky they just happen one at a time but sometimes they all happen at once. He is a walking Lemony Snicket.

'My eye is watering. Can you see my eye watering?' he said. 'What if my eye is leaking brain fluid? Are brains made of fluid? How much fluid can I afford to lose?'

'George, I'm not a doctor but I suspect your eye is watering because you just stuck a drumstick in it,' I said.

'Right, right, yes, that would make sense, I did do that,' said George. 'I'm fine. Everything is fine. My brains are most likely not leaking out of my eye.'

I had totally reassured George.

WOAH YEAH!

(Hey, steady on, choir of angels. I have to reassure him every half an hour or so. It's no biggie.)

Naomi was standing by her amplifier, her

bass guitar hanging at the coolest angle you can imagine. She stared into space. I don't know how she does it, but even standing doing nothing she looks like an album cover or a selfie with a million likes. She is *so* cool.

I plugged my amp in. I didn't have a microphone because I couldn't afford one. Mum always says I don't need one anyway because my voice is so amazing. What she actually says is, 'Please, lower your voice a bit, there's people on the moon trying to sleep,' but she *means* it's amazing.

'OK,' I said. 'Shall we do "Alpaca Waka Waka"?'

As well as being in charge of naming the band, and the chords we play, I am also in charge of naming the songs. I think you can see why.

'Alpaca Waka Waka' was the new song I had written that morning, and the new chord I had made up for it was F minus.

'Right, George, on four bang the biscuit tin and Naomi, hit that string there.' I pointed at the string I wanted her to play.

23

These are the things you have to do when you're the main person in a band. It's hard work but very rewarding.

I arranged my fingers on the guitar's fretboard in the shape of F minus. It felt good. It felt right.

'A-one, a-two, a-one two three FOUR!'

George banged the Tupperware, Naomi twanged the bass, and I hit the strings of my guitar and shouted **'ALPACA!'** because that's the words of the song.

SKA-DANNNNNNNNNNG!

WHAT THE HECK WAS THAT?

It was awful. It was so bad I almost imagined I saw a weird floating set of double doors marked 'WAY OUT' appear out of thin air right in front of me.

The thing is, in Normalton, you sometimes saw weird things appearing and disappearing, and the Biscuit Factory was very clear that if you saw something like that then you should a) forget about it and b) forget you forgot about it, which is why I never said anything about those weird double doors at the time. They would turn out to be quite important later in the story though, so don't a) forget I mentioned it and then b) forget you forgot.

'WHAT THE HECK WAS THAT?' I said. 'That is NOT what I said to play. George, why d'you hit the Tupperware? I told you to hit the biscuit tin. And Naomi, wrong string! Wrong string!'

'Awwwww *heck*,' said George. 'My f-f-f-fillings are trying to jump out of my mouth! They're v-v-v-vibrating!'

'Can we try that again, the way I said to do it?'

'And d-d-did anyone else see a f-f-floating d—' said George, but it was time for him to stop speaking and start playing again and he obviously hadn't realised that, so I helped him out by counting in to the song.

'Ready? A-one, a-two, a-one two three FOUR!'

SKA-DANNNNNNNNNG!
'ALPACA!'

WOAH!

Then some interesting things happened.

25

Firstly, I got vexed, really truly vexed because **'SKA-DANNNNNG'** was not the noise I wanted to hear, which meant that either George or Naomi had played it wrong *again*. Secondly, for a couple of seconds I definitely, *totally* saw a weird floating set of double doors marked 'WAY OUT' appear out of thin air right in front of me, which then flickered and disappeared. And thirdly:

KRRRRRRRRAAAAAAAAKKKKSH!

'That's not the right noise either!' I said.

'Ahem,' said Naomi. I looked over. A large block of plaster had fallen from the ceiling and landed about a metre away from her. Obviously, she hadn't shouted, or moved. She was too cool for that.

'How did that happen?' asked George. 'And did anyone else see a floating d—'

Then: *KRRRRRRRRAAAAAAAAKKKKSH!*

Another chunk of ceiling fell, narrowly missing George this time.

'What the . . .?'

Something was really clattering the roof of the Community Centre.

I unstrapped my guitar and rushed outside, closely followed by George and Naomi.

There was another **KRRRRRAAAAKKKKSH!**

We looked up.

'Oh,' said George.

Normalton Community Centre has a lot of really great features that make it perfect for band practice. It has toilets and plug sockets and Wi-Fi and a vending machine that sells pickled-onion-flavoured things.

Right now it also had a really, REALLY tall, really, REALLY orange, really, REALLY furry monster flailing at it with really, REALLY long, furry orange arms.

Really.

Chapter 4

EEEEEK

Biscuit Factory Emergency Protocols

Biscuit Factory Emergency Protocols such as
quarantining, Biscuitron mobilisation and driving
our mysterious-looking vans around corners too
quickly so they make a *squeeeeee* noise with their
tyres etc. are enacted at the point where an anomaly
is detected. As anomalies are never detected (see
<u>Anomalies</u>), Biscuit Factory Emergency Protocols
are never enacted. If you see one of our mysterious-
looking vans *squeeeeee*ing around a corner it's
probably because we're late for tea or are chasing a
round biscuit (e.g. digestive, rich tea, custard cream
with the corners bitten off) that is rolling down a hill —
those things can go quite fast.

[extracted from *Biccypedia*]

The creature flapped its fuzzy arms at the roof of the hut, knocking tiles, guttering and a frisbee I hadn't seen for two summers to the ground. We stood and stared for a few tense seconds, seconds which seemed to stretch time just long enough for me to tell you what the thing actually looked like.

YOU HAVE 1 NEW NOTIFICATION:
A PRECISE AND ACCURATE DESCRIPTION
OF THE MONSTER

Oh, it was tall. Really, really tall. Like, really tall, you know? It was . . . oh, how shall I put this? It was super-tall.

It was also orange. Really, really orange, etc. etc. If you want to picture how orange it was imagine an orange, that should help.

So, to recap, this was a tall, orange monster, with a huge, round body and a smaller, round head, and round, red eyes, all shiny like plastic picnic plates. All this was balanced on two long, thin legs. Below its knobbly knees

**its shins were completely covered in orange
feathers which obscured its feet. It looked
like it was walking around on two gimongous
upside-down feather dusters.**

**What I'm basically saying is: the absolute
state of this . . . this . . . Bumblefluff, honestly.
And that's before it opened its mouth, which
it was just about to do . . .**

The creature opened its mouth and drew a
breath with a noise like a gale whistling round a
deserted high street, only backwards.

'I'M MAKING A BIG NOISE!' it bellowed in a
deep, loud, rumbly voice. 'WITH MY MOUTH!'

'What?' I said, because *What*?

'MOVE ALONG!' said a different voice.

I turned to see a tall, thin man wearing beige
Biscuit Factory overalls standing right next to
me. He had a long, narrow nose which made his
face look like it was pointing at me, and he was
holding a megaphone. On his chest was a badge
which read: 'Hi, I'm Blankley. Ask me about our

Double-Nutty Nibbles!'

'NOTHING TO SEE HERE.'

I stared at him in disbelief.

And the Biscuit Factory air-raid siren went off again.

WOOOOOOOOOOOOOOOOO!

Well, of course this was the fault of the Biscuit Factory.

And then, just because there wasn't enough going on at this precise moment, George lost his chill completely.

'Heck!' said George. 'Heck! Heck!'

'George, don't overreact,' I said.

George was walking round in a tight little circle, flapping his hands up and down. A total lack of chill. And you might say: 'All right, Captain Harsh, come on. There's a carrot-coloured monster over there. Let George have his moment.' And you almost have a point but not really and also this is my book, so shush.

'I'M HITTING THIS BRICK BOX,' bellowed the creature. 'WITH MY ORANGE FIST!'

'Heck!' said George again. 'Monster!' he added.

'George, come on, it's OK,' I said. 'We'll just practise somewhere else.'

'What?' said George. It was an improvement. At least he wasn't screaming.

The thing is, when you live in Normalton, weird things are going to happen because of the Biscuit Factory.

YOU HAVE 1 NEW NOTIFICATION: WHAT'S ALL THIS ABOUT THE BISCUIT FACTORY THEN?

Let me be clear.

Whatever the chumps who work in the 'Biscuit Factory' say they are doing, it's a fairly open secret around town that they keep tearing holes in the fabric of reality. We all know this because strange things keep tumbling out of those holes and making our lives a bit more difficult and vexing than they need to be.

Like the time we were invaded by The Clouds

of Disapproval, a slow-moving weather front of greenish puffs of condensed water vapour that floated across Normalton looking down on us all and making rude personal comments about us as we passed by.

'Where d'you get that jacket from, the rubbish jacket shop?' they would sniff.

Or, 'I love what you've done with your make-up. The colour-blind clown look is bang on trend these days.'

Or, 'What's stupid and wet? You!' and then they would rain on us.

I mean, talk about whatever the opposite of 'funny weather' is. These clouds were properly unhilarious. And around twice a month another bit of annoying weirdness would float around town, we'd ignore it, it would disappear, repeat, repeat, repeat.

How does the 'Biscuit Factory' get away with it? They have an utterly genius strategy: they simply flat-out deny any of it actually happens. And the people of Normalton go along with it. It's a weird game that grown-ups seem to enjoy playing.

So whenever the air-raid siren goes off, and a massively visible bit of extra-dimensional nonsense hits the town, we either stay in until it's gone away, or go out and try our hardest to ignore it. That's just what we do. It's just normal.

'PLEASE MOVE AWAY FROM THE BUILDING,' said Blankley.

'Oh wait, hey, no, we were having a band practice,' I said. 'So we'll have to pop back in there to get our stuff if that's OK.'

Blankley was faster than he looked, because before I'd got more than two steps towards the building he was in my way, and in my face with his megaphone.

'BAND PRACTICE IS CANCELLED,' he said, the combination of his nasal voice and the megaphone making his voice sound like a snide anteater shouting in a big tin box.

'Yes, I mean, no, it's postponed, I get that,' I said, 'but as I was explaining, El Jirafa Tremendo is in there, so—'

'PLEASE OBEY THE SIGN,' said Blankley.

'What sign?' I said, because the only sign outside the Community Centre was a sign that said 'Community Centre' and how do you obey that? But then Blankley pointed in the direction of a brand-new sign I had never seen before that said:

CAUTION: IF YOU CAN READ THIS SIGN YOU SHOULD GO HOME NOW. THANKS.

'We'd better do what the sign says, Hadz,' said George nervously. He is a big believer in doing what he is told, which is good sometimes, i.e. when I'm telling him what to do, but bad at other times, i.e. this time.

'We are not doing what the sign says, George. Naomi, tell him,' I said, looking for a bit of support. 'Naomi?'

Naomi was being typical Naomi, too cool to take any notice of anything that was going on. In fact, she had managed to position herself so she was facing away from the monster, and from Blankley and, most baffling of all, from me.

And for a moment I forgot about the mayhem around me and just admired the sheer 'not even bothered' attitude of my bass player.

She's so cool.

Sometimes I wish I wasn't even bothered. It would make my life a lot quieter, and it would mean I was a lot cooler, just mooching about, looking amazing, doing nothing, being not even bothered in a variety of locations around town. But the creator of the universe saw fit to make me totally bothered. And when I am bothered, I stay bothered until whatever is bothering me has been sorted. And if I have to sort it, then sort it I shall! Because I hate feeling bothered, which is a shame because sometimes it feels like I am BOTHERED ALL THE TIME. And it might not be cool but at least it keeps things interesting.

'YOU THERE. NO LOITERING. MOVE ALONG. NOTHING TO SEE.'

'Why are you shouting at me? There's a furry

satsuma fighting the Community Centre! Shout at that,' I shouted at Blankley, as the big, fuzzy Bumblefluff took another swing at the roof.

'NO, THERE ISN'T!' he said into his megaphone.

'WE'RE HITTING THIS BUILDING. WEEEEEE!' said a loud, rumbly voice behind us.

As Blankley eyeballed me ferociously, I pointedly turned to look at the monster, so he could see that I could see what I could see. But what I could see was not exactly what I expected to see, so I turned back to him.

'I apologise. You're right,' I said. 'There isn't a large, orange furry thing going all Royal Rumble with the roof. There are two large, orange furry things going all Royal Rumble with the roof.'

'WHAT?' said Blankley. He looked at the building. 'Eeeeeeek!' he added.

It's hard to say whether that was an overreaction, but there were now two gargantuan orange things slapping the Community Centre with their ridiculous fat paws.

Chapter 5

WOMWOMWOM

Recipes

Recipes are instructions you follow when you want to cook something, like a biscuit. If anyone asks you about the recipes of any of our biscuits it would probably be best if you pretend to faint, pretend you don't understand English or pretend to explode (this will only work if you are really good at pretending).

[extracted from *Biccypedia*]

Blankley's jaw dropped. His left eye twitched. He nervously licked his lips.

'Oh heck. Oh hecky heck. Oh heck,' he said. 'This is . . . this is . . . OK, come on you can do this. Breathe.'

'I am breathing,' I said. 'I always breathe. It's like a thing I do literally all day.'

'WOAH YEAH!' sang the choir of angels in my head, because *that* was funny.

'Will you be quiet for a moment,' said Blankley. 'I'm trying to . . . I'm trying to . . . wait, I know.'

He raised his left arm so his sleeve was right next to his mouth.

'Code Five. We have a Code Five,' said Blankley into his sleeve. 'All units please converge on Community Centre.'

'What's a Code Five?' I asked.

'What?' he said. He looked shifty for a moment, then he smiled like a tiger would if it saw a slow-moving gazelle wrapped in bacon, i.e. a bad smile.

He bent over so his face was right in mine. He nearly took my eye out with his nose.

'I didn't say anything about a Code Five, little

39

girl,' he said. 'You must have mis-heard.'

'Sir, did you say Code Five, sir?' came a crackly voice from his sleeve. *'Sir, please repeat, did you say Code Five? It sounded like Code Five, sir, is that what you said, sir? Please confirm, is this a Code Five situation, sir?'*

His smile never wavered. I countered with a smile of my own, the sweet, innocent smile of someone who knows that they shouldn't be smiling right now because it will really annoy the person they are smiling at, i.e. the best kind of smile. I would have fluttered my eyelashes, too, but that would have been overdoing it.

'Little girl, I want to make it clear that there's no such thing as a Code Five. And also you never heard me say anything about a Code Five, because I never said it. Because I couldn't have said it because I'm not even here. Do I make myself clear?' he said.

'Sir,' came the crackly voice from his sleeve. *'Sir, are you saying there's no such thing as a Code Five? Because we're all wearing our Code*

40

Five safety gear, sir, and we've got into our Code Five van and if there's no such thing as a Code Five, sir, then how come we have the safety gear and the van, sir? Also, why are you calling me a little girl? Is that a code, sir?'

'What if we promise not to notice there are two monsters out here,' I said, pointedly ignoring the voices coming from the man's sleeve, 'and promise not to notice you and your team Code Five-ing around the place, please could we just go in and get our stuff?'

'Sir, Susan has her Code Five wellies on, sir, should she take them off, sir?' came the crackly voice from the man's sleeve.

'Will you please stop talking for a moment!' shouted Blankley into his sleeve. He either had a concealed microphone up there, or there was a group of tiny, confused people with tinny voices living in his armpit. The way today was going it was hard to be 100 per cent sure which was the most likely.

'You,' he said, jabbing his finger at me. 'I can't

deal with you right now.'

I get that a lot.

He marched over towards George.

'If you'd just let us get our stuff I promise we'll go away,' I said to his back, but he wasn't listening.

He reached George and leaned threateningly over him, pushing his face right into George's airspace.

George did not enjoy confrontations with authority. He spent all his time at school trying to perfect the art of being invisible to anyone over the age of thirteen. If a teacher, or a dinner lady, or even a particularly tall classroom gerbil so much as looked at him he would start juddering like a phone on vibrate.

'You, boy,' said Blankley.

'Eeek. Oh no. I'm sorry,' stuttered George. 'Is my face in your way? I can move it, if you'd like. I could, I could put it somewhere else. In a shoebox or or or . . .'

'Are you a good boy?' said Blankley.

'I . . . I . . . I . . . yes. I am. I'm a good boy. Good

boy, George,' said George, with a desperate smile. 'Did I get the question right? Can we stop talking now?'

'If you are a good boy, you need to get on the bus and go home, and you need to take your two friends with you,' said Blankley, pointing at me. 'Will you do that?'

'Um . . . I mean . . . who bus? What two? Home what? Yes?' said George.

'You and her,' said Blankley, pointing very rudely at me with both his finger and his nose, which was double-rude when you think about it. 'And her . . . uh, where's the other one gone?'

I looked around. Naomi was nowhere to be seen. There was a pile of soil where she had been standing ignoring us five minutes ago. She'd probably moved to get away from the soil – soil and cool clothes do not mix. Even so, I couldn't help feeling a little disappointed that she'd abandoned us. Friends should stick together.

'Good,' said Blankley. 'Just two of you to deal with. Are you getting on the bus?' he said to

George. 'Or do we have a problem?'

'Oh! Well, no. No problem. George no problem!' said George. 'But, I mean . . . what bus?'

'I'll take that as a yes,' said Blankley.

'OK! No problem,' beamed George, happy to have made Blankley happy.

'Woah, hey, I'm not going without El Jirafa,' I said. 'Also, what bus?'

'Splendid,' said Blankley. 'I'll take that as a yes, too. Everything is under control. All totally sorted. Everyone's getting on the bus.'

He rubbed his hands together in a 'job done' gesture, looked towards the Community Centre and said 'Eeeeeeeeeek!' again.

Because there were now five giant orange things gathered around the building.

'Where are all these things coming from?' he wailed.

At that moment there was a small sound, like **womwomwom**, and all the little hairs on my arms stood on end as a large set of double doors appeared out of nowhere next to the

Community Centre.

They were perfectly normal doors, really, with a sign sellotaped to them reading: 'Please use other door'. The only weird thing about them was all the lime-green crackles of lightning that danced around the frame, and the fact they were floating around a metre from the ground, and the fact that when they opened, another super-tall, orange, furry monster squeezed out of them.

The monster was way too big for the doorway it was coming through but that didn't stop it. Watching it happen made my eyes and my brain hurt. It was like seeing a ginormous fluffy bubble being blown out of a door-shaped bubble maker. A bit.

When the monster had fully emerged, the door disappeared with a barely perceptible *mowmowmow* and the monster stretched.

We stared at it for a few moments. Then it opened its wide, dark mouth and said, 'WHY DON'T YOU TAKE A PHOTO? IT'LL LAST LONGER.'

'OK, that's it. Get on the bus,' said Blankley, as a large red bus pulled up on the road between us and the monster-infested Community Centre.

Chapter 6

SHHHHH

The bus was as big as a bus and as red as a bus and as reassuring as a bus.

YOU HAVE 1 NEW NOTIFICATION:
A MESSAGE ABOUT BUSES

Buses are great. Buses are solid and dependable and regular. They are like a rectangle on wheels and what's more trustworthy than a rectangle? You really know where you are with a bus, usually because the driver will tell you where you are, if you ask them. 'Where are we?' you'd ask. 'The beginning of chapter six,' she'd reply. 'Are you getting off here?'

I'd recommend you stay on. Chapter seven is pretty good.

If anything, this bus was even more reassuring than a normal bus because it had the words 'EVERYTHING IS ALL RIGHT!' written on its side in big, friendly lettering.

It was an open-topped double-decker, the kind that takes tourists around big cities so they can take selfies in front of big clocks, haunted pubs and hotels that King George the Regular once did a majestic poo in. Weirdly, nobody was sitting on the top deck. I couldn't see into the lower deck because the windows were tinted.

EVERYTHING IS ALL RIGHT!

I stared at the words for a while. I had never been lied to by a bus before, at least as far as I could remember, so maybe . . . maybe everything *was* all right. But then I remembered that behind the bus there were monsters being annoying and a man stopping me from having a band practice, which didn't seem very all right to me.

'Everything is all right,' said George. He was staring at the bus. There was something weird about his face. There were no worry lines on his forehead. There was a hint of a smile on his lips.

'George,' I said. 'What's wrong?'

'Nothing,' he said.

That's what was weird – with George there was always something wrong, something worrying him.

'Everything is all right,' he murmured, and he sounded like he meant it. This bus was *super-*

reassuring. It had helped George find his chill.

'George, I'm not sure—'

Shhhhhhhh.

I had been interrupted by the sound of the bus door opening. Standing in the doorway was a woman with a winning smile. As she spoke to us her eyes twinkled and her dimples dimpled. She was *delightful*.

'Hey, you guys, I'm Jill,' she said, her voice like warm, smooth chocolate. And the badge on her chest agreed with her. 'Hi, I'm Jill. Ask me about our Chocoberry Chomps!' it said.

'Are you feeling anxious? Vexed? That must be very tiring. Why not get on the Happybus and we'll take you home.'

'How is getting on this bus going to solve my problems?' I said. 'My problems are really big and orange and annoying.'

Jill, who was wearing Biscuit Factory overalls, smiled a smile that couldn't have been more likeable if it was made out of sleepy puppies. 'We've got a vending machine that sells pickled-onion-flavoured things, and every seat has a screen in front of it. We are currently showing a box set of *Big-Sword Vampire Pet Shop Owner* which is, like, super-motto.'

'I like super-motto things,' murmured George under his breath. 'Sometimes things that are just motto aren't motto enough.' He was stepping slowly towards the bus as if he was in a dream. Not a great dream, obviously. A dream where you walk slowly towards a bus wouldn't be in my top ten dreams but then it is an easy dream to have come true, which this one was, for George, if he *had* ever dreamed of walking slowly towards a bus ... which ...

Anyway. He was walking slowly towards the bus.

... but actually maybe this WAS a dream come true for George. Maybe it was a dream come true for a lot of people. Here, step inside this bus, and don't worry about anything, because everything is all right.

But everything isn't all right.

But wouldn't it be nice if we could pretend it was?

Wouldn't it be nice if I could pretend it was?

It would.

But I can't.

YOU HAVE 1 NEW NOTIFICATION:
A MESSAGE ABOUT PRETENDING
EVERYTHING IS ALL RIGHT

One time I was cosily tucked up in bed on a cold winter's night. I didn't want to leave the warm, nurturing cocoon of my Sleepy Sloth duvet.

But I also needed the toilet. Quite badly. I had drunk mucho hot chocolate that evening. Mistakes had been made.

But I was also quite sleepy. And warm. And cosy.

But I knew really that I could do with going to the toilet before I went to sleep.

But it was cold outside and warm in here.

So I decided to unleash the power of my

imagination and imagine that if I didn't go to the toilet and just went back to sleep, everything would be all right.

I did. It wasn't.

I woke up with an in-duvet climate catastrophe on my hands. Rising waters. You get the picture.

And now imagine it's someone else wetting YOUR bed and trying to tell you everything's all right.

And since then I have been unable to pretend that everything is all right when it isn't.

I also drink less hot chocolate just before bed.

(Is this the ickiest thing you ever read? Hope so! Bet you're glad now that you didn't get off the bus at the beginning of this chapter.)

'Come on, Hadz,' George said. 'Let's eat some snacks and watch some anime.'

He was already halfway through the bus's door.

'George, hang on a sec,' I said.

'Everything is all right,' he said, as he walked past Jill and disappeared on to the bus.

Jill smiled at me, a smile so bright and warm you could get a slight tan from it.

'Come on in,' she said.

'But . . . I need to get my guitar,' I said.

'Can't that wait till later? Your friends are all on the Happybus,' said Jill, smiling.

I looked at that smile, and at the words on the side of the bus.

EVERYTHING IS ALL RIGHT!

Maybe I *could* get my guitar later. This problem would soon be sorted out anyway. They even had a name for it. 'Code Five.' You give something a name so you can sort it out. Somewhere in the Biscuit Factory there'd be a poster or a pamphlet telling everyone how to deal with a Code Five. Soon Susan would be here, in her Code Five wellies, sorting out the Code Five problems, and then me and George and Naomi could forget it ever happened, and we could start playing once more.

Which reminded me.

'Wait,' I said. 'Where's Naomi? We should wait for her.'

Because where the heck had Naomi gone?

'Come on,' said Jill again. 'Get on the bus.'

Fine, I thought. Naomi would no doubt turn up later, looking cool. That was something to look forward to, at least. And in the meantime I'd probably better stick with George.

'Just so you know,' I said to her as I walked towards the bus, 'I persuaded *myself* to get on this bus.'

'That's all right,' said Jill, stepping to one side to let me pass. 'Everything is all right.'

'Is it?' I said. 'Is it really though?'

Shhhhhh! said the Happybus.

Chapter 7

DOOBY DOOBY DA

Answers

Did you mean: **everything** is all right?
The page 'Answers' does not exist. You can <u>ask for it to be created</u>, but consider checking whether the thing with two mouths crawling towards you is actually real or whether you might actually just be imagining it. It's really quite close to you now, so you should know one way or another pretty soon.

[extracted from *Biccypedia*]

The doors closed behind me.

The interior of the bus was warm and dimly

lit. It smelled like one of my mum's candles, the ones she'd light after she'd had to make a phone call or answer the door. Candles with names like 'Ocean Mist' or 'Mmmm Caramel' or 'Afternoon Nap'. The overall effect was cosy and calming.

'Sit yourself down,' beamed Jill, gesturing at the seats. 'And I'll get us all where we need to be.'

I scanned the orderly rows of plushly upholstered seats looking for a smallish, sandy-haired bag of worry, i.e. George. I couldn't see one. I looked again and saw something that was definitely the size and shape and colour of George, but it was smiling serenely like it was at peace with the world, which was something you didn't see very often. He looked happy. This wouldn't do at all. I went to sit next to him.

'Here's the plan,' I said, sinking into a seat that felt warm and fluffy, like parking your bum on a dozing panda. It practically sighed as I sat. 'Once we're off this stupid bus we'll head back to band practice.'

'Are you sure?' said George dreamily. 'I think

we're supposed to go home.'

'No, we're supposed to be having a band practice.'

'Shhhhh,' he said, sounding like the door of a bus. *'Big-Sword Vampire Pet Shop Owner* is on and, Haddie? It's exactly as motto as Jill said it would be.'

He stared at the blue-haired, heavily armed schoolgirl who was bouncing around making robot wereweasels explode on the screen in front of him.

'But, George . . .'

'How is everything?' called Jill from the front of the bus.

'Everything is all right!' shouted the passengers happily, including George.

'That's right!' laughed Jill as I gave George a kind-of-friendly but also kind-of-hard punch in the bicep.

'Stop saying everything's all right,' I said. 'How can you be so calm? Naomi's missing and we're not having a band practice right now.'

Shhhhhh.

'Don't you shush me. Oh heckit, it was the door again, wasn't it?'

The bus had stopped, and three passengers were walking down the aisle towards the open doorway.

There was a pop and a whine – I recognised the sound of somebody switching on a microphone.

Jill started to sing:

'Go straight into your house,

'And shut the door up tight,

'And sit there feeling good,

'Cos everything's all right.

'Come on, everyone! Join in!' she shouted, and even though she wasn't facing us you could tell she was smiling a smile so wide the top of her face was probably in danger of falling off.

That song was infuriating. For many (four) reasons:

1) It was not true.

2) Everyone was joining in with it anyway.

3) Jill's voice was so heckin' lovely that it almost made me want to join in.

And finally:

4) It had made me write a list and I absolutely despise writing lists. I'd tell you all the reasons why I hate writing lists but . . . well, you see my problem.

Shhhhh went the bus door as it closed, and I felt like it was shushing my brain specifically. And then Jill sang again.

'We're riding in a bus
'And everything's all right!
'And something something else,
'And everything's all right!'

Everybody on the bus was happily singing along as though they knew the words already. Even though the bus was almost full I felt alone and vexed, too vexed to be near anyone at this point, including George, so I stood up to try and find another seat. I don't think he even noticed me leaving as he sang and watched anime.

'La la la la la,

'And everything's all right!

'And dooby dooby da,

'And everything's all right!'

I thought looking out of a window might help but they were so tinted it was difficult to see through them. Then I remembered this was an open-topped double-decker so I headed for the stairs.

The stairs were gated, and the gate was bolted shut. I gave it a shake, and then another shake. It wouldn't open.

'Sit yourself back down!'

I had been so intent on opening the gate I hadn't noticed the bus had stopped and Jill was standing right over me.

I looked up in shock. Her big, delightful face was all smiles, by which I mean she still had a big smile on her face, not that she had lots of small ones all over, because that wouldn't have looked quite so affable.

'And everything's all right!' she sang at me.

'I just want some air,' I said.

'Seriously, little girl, sit back down and sing the song or we're going to have a serious problem,' hissed Jill, her smile never wavering.

'*And everything's all right!*' she added.

I had to get off this bus. I needed a distraction.

'Listen, Jill, I'm trying to sing along and I know everything's all right, but there's someone on this bus who doesn't believe everything's all right and he's refusing to sing and he's making me feel like maybe everything isn't all right after all,' I said.

'Oh, sweetheart. Point them out to me,' smiled Jill. 'It's very important that everybody believes that everything's all right, because if everybody doesn't believe that everything's all right then . . . well, we just have to change their minds, don't we?'

'It's him!' I cried, pointing at George.

Everyone on the bus turned to face George. And George noticed and his face went from a picture of serene calm to intense worry in a split second.

That was the George I knew and loved! It was good to see him back, looking ever more stressed as the passengers stared and Jill advanced on him.

Now everyone's attention was on George I was able to walk calmly to the front of the bus, where the 'open door' button was.

'Hey, stop right there,' shouted Jill.

Shhhhhh said the bus door as it opened.

I couldn't have said it better myself, so I said nothing and quickly stepped off the bus.

'Thank goodness for that,' said a man lying on the pavement right in front of me. 'I was getting a bit worried there.'

'I AM SITTING ON THIS MAN,' said the large, orange creature who was sitting on the man.

I briefly considered getting back on the Happybus.

Chapter 8

HAHA

Ingredients

Ingredients are the things we combine to make biscuits. If you see a box in the Biscuit Factory marked 'Danger: Radioactive' or 'Caution: Mad Science Equipment' or 'Do not open if you don't want your face to almost certainly melt off accidentally', instead of being alarmed, just consider that maybe somebody misspelled 'ingredients'. But also definitely do not open the box.

[extracted from *Biccypedia*]

But I didn't get back on the Happybus. Outside the Happybus was the opposite of inside the

Happybus. Out here was real life. I could feel the wind on my face, and I could smell car exhaust and overfull litter bins, and I could see the sky and some shops and a man on the ground being sat on by a monster.

It wasn't ideal but it was better than the weird atmosphere of the Happybus, that's for sure.

Some kinds of weird are easier to deal with than others.

Shhhhhh said the Happybus door as it closed behind me.

The man on the ground was Tony Aroma. He ran Normalton's Gym and Fitness Centre, and he was very muscly indeed. You would see him marching around town with his tight T-shirt looking like it was stuffed full of basketballs. Strong as he was, he was utterly helpless beneath the creature that was sitting on his legs.

'Are you OK?' I said to him.

'Oh, yes, yes, sorry,' he said. 'Everything is all right, thank you.'

Oh for pity's sake, I thought to myself.

'You do realise there's a giant orange monster sitting on you, don't you?'

'Oh, I doubt that.'

See, this is what really hecked me off about Normalton. Everybody knew that the Biscuit Factory was a Super-Secret Science Lab in disguise, everybody knew that they kept having accidents up there, everybody knew that those accidents meant that weird stuff would happen around town, and yet absolutely everybody pretended to ignore that weird stuff. Even if that weird stuff was huge and orange and actually sitting on them.

I knew there was no point in trying to convince Tony that everything was, in fact, pretty far from all right but then on the other hand I couldn't just let him lie there, so instead I grabbed his arm and gave it a tug.

I heaved and heaved but he didn't budge an inch.

'Morning, Tony!'

It was Mrs Missis, who worked in Coolbeans!,

66

one of Normalton's seven coffee shops with 'beans' in their name, probably on her way to work.

'Morning, Mrs Missis,' said Tony.

'Lovely weather, isn't it,' said Mrs Missis, carefully walking round the orange monster that was blocking the pavement.

'Can't complain!' said Tony.

This whole conversation took place as I was straining, teeth gritted, trying single-handedly to drag Tony out from under the big orange Bumblefluff.

'Mrs Missis, I don't suppose you could give me a hand here, could you?'

'Of course. What with?'

Shhhhh.

Oh great, that was the Happybus door opening. Still, maybe Jill would give me a hand.

'Oh hey, guys, so I was thinking you'd like to get on the Happybus now, what do you say?'

'What me?' said Mrs Missis.

'Absolutely you,' smiled Jill. 'You wouldn't be

on the Happybus if you weren't on the Happybus now, would you?'

Mrs Missis frowned slightly as she tried to work out exactly what it was that Jill had said. Then she shook her head.

'I suppose not,' she laughed, and on to the Happybus she stepped.

'I don't think Tony will be getting on the Happybus,' I said.

'Haha, why ever not?' said Jill. The 'haha' wasn't a laugh exactly, just that every word in that sentence seemed to contain a laugh, a joyful, friendly laugh that was really starting to get on my nerves.

'Because he's stuck under a monster!' I said.

'Oh, I doubt that,' laughed Jill.

'Haha, that's what I said,' said Tony.

'I AM SITTING ON THIS MAN,' said the monster, but nobody took any notice.

'So are you getting on the Happybus or what?' said Jill.

'Absolutely!' said Tony. 'I'm getting on that

Happybus and nothing's going to stop me!'

Shhhhhh.

You might think that was me, or Jill, or the disembodied voice of the rational universe shushing Tony for saying something so ridiculous but of course it wasn't, it was the Happybus door opening and the reason it was opening was because I'd pushed the 'open door' button.

The conversation between Tony and Jill was clearly going nowhere, and it looked like it was going to take a while to get there, so I had taken the opportunity to pop back on the Happybus and grab George and take him on an adventure, i.e. to the Community Centre to restart our band practice.

I walked down the aisle to George, stood by his seat and held out my hand.

'Now's our chance to blow this joint,' I said. It was a truly fabooly moment for me personally, as I had never had such a perfect opportunity to say 'blow this joint' before.

WOAH YEAH!

Shhhhhh.

The closing of the Happybus door shushed the choir of angels, which was just typical of this Happybus's attitude really, when you thought about it.

I stood there for a bit, hand outstretched.

And George ignored me. To be fair he had the air of somebody ignoring everything. He was staring at the back of the seat in front of him, not at the screen, and the look on his face was . . . blank. Not anxious, not happy. Not anything. It was like someone had pressed his soft reset button, and his face was back to factory defaults.

'George, come on,' I said, waggling my hand a little in case he hadn't seen it.

'Go away,' he said quietly.

'Is this because I pointed at you and made everybody look at you and then Jill came over and started telling you off, which is like all your worst nightmares coming true at once?'

He said nothing.

'Because I had to do it, George, so I could get off the Happybus.'

He said nothing.

'So I'm forgiven, is what I'm saying.'

George shook his head slowly.

'You are such a Vinny Vacuum,' he said.

My blood ran a bit cold and I dropped my hand. I didn't know exactly what he meant by that, but it certainly didn't sound good.

'Are you saying . . . what are you saying? Are you saying . . . I suck? Like a vacuum cleaner?'

I sat down next to him.

'Hadz, it's worse than that. You're all smiles and bright colours and the promise of fun but sometimes . . . sometimes being with you is just hard work.'

'But we do fun, cool things. We're in a band. Which is why we've got to get off this Happybus and go to practice!'

'I think I'd better stay here if that's OK.'

'George, listen, you can't just stay here because someone told you to.'

'I dunno if you've noticed but being in a band with you involves being told what to do all the time. I'm used to it.'

'Well that's . . . I mean that's not . . .'

I stood up, confused. I looked around at all the people on the bus, quietly sitting looking at their screens. All of them ignoring what was happening outside. Then I realised exactly what was going on. It was the Biscuit Factory doing this! Of course it was! It was brainwashing them, or maybe hypnotising them, or something.

'George! This Happybus is getting to you, George. It's the warmth, and the comfy chairs, and the singing. They've brainwashed you. I insist you come with me off this Happybus. It's for your own good!'

'Is it?' said George. 'Or is it for *your* own good?'

'Oh, poor George. They've really got to you. I'll tell you what. If you really want to stay on this bus . . .?'

'And I do,' he said quietly.

'Then that is fine by me,' I said nobly. 'You can

get dropped off at home. I'm going to go and get my guitar, and then I'll come to your house and totally rescue you, and then we'll go and finish our band practice.'

George was staring at me. I couldn't work out his expression exactly, but it was something close to amazement, I think.

Which was exactly the right expression because I was being amazing.

WOAH YEAH!

George turned his head away from me so he was looking at the darkly tinted window, probably so I wouldn't see the single tear of gratitude that was most likely dribbling down his freckly face right at that moment.

'I'll be back,' I said.

WOAH YEAH!

And then I got the heck off that bus.

Chapter 9

WAAAAAAAAH

Calm Down

Occasionally the people of Normalton will get a little overexcited. Do not tell them to **Calm Down**. Nobody ever calmed down because somebody told them to calm down (see also <u>Cheer Up</u> and <u>Don't Panic</u>). If you see a member of the public in danger of non-calm behaviours simply direct them to read the side of the nearest bus, where we have placed calming and distracting messages about upcoming films/exciting household products/promises that everything will be all right, etc.

[extracted from *Biccypedia*]

'Everything's all right,

   'Cos everything's all right,

   'Everything's all right

   'Cos everything's all right.'

Not much had changed outside, except that Jill and Tony were loudly singing on the pavement, and also now there was a big orange monster sitting on Jill.

I couldn't help myself.

'Shouldn't you be on the bus, Jill?'

'I'll be on there in two shakes of a duck's face,' smiled Jill.

'Of course you will,' I beamed back. 'Good to see everything's all right!'

'That's right!' said Jill.

I had choices at this moment. I could have stayed to try and help Jill and Tony, and possibly I should have, but how do you help people who are so convinced that everything's all right that they won't even help themselves?

You can't.

So to heck with them, I thought.

And while I was at it, to heck with the Biscuit Factory! They had brainwashed George, they had somehow made Naomi disappear and they had separated me from El Jirafa Tremendo, which was a lot like separating me from my left arm, only I suppose less painful and involving less blood but even so! I was going to rescue El Jirafa Tremendo and have a band practice all by myself. And that was just fine by me.

Womwomwom.

I recognised that sound.

All the little hairs on my arms stood on end as a large set of double doors appeared out of nowhere right beside me.

They were perfectly normal doors, really, with a sign sellotaped to them reading: 'Please use other door'. The only weird thing about them was all the lime-green crackles of lightning that danced around the frame, and the fact they were floating around a metre from the ground, and the fact that when they opened a massive, orange furry monster squeezed out of them.

No matter how many times I saw the exact same thing happen, in the exact same way, it didn't get any less weird.

The monster would have landed right on me if I hadn't stepped smartly to one side.

'And that's the difference between me and the rest of you,' I said to nobody in particular. 'When I see a big orange monster squeezing out of a large set of weird floating double doors, I get out of the way.'

'What door?' said Tony.

'What monster?' said Jill.

I left them to it and went to get my guitar.

The walk through town was relatively uneventful. Every two minutes or so there'd be a **womwomwom** and some doors would appear and a monster would squeeze out but from what I could tell, as long as the creature didn't actually land on you, they were no bother. They would just stand there looking ridiculous and saying obvious things and let's face it, you do that all the time, don't you? And you're no bother, mostly.

The things that could have caused me bother were the prowling Happybuses. I spotted the first one on the corner of Orderly Street. I crouched behind a parked car and watched as a smiling bus driver ushered compliant townspeople on to the bus with a rousing chorus of 'Everything's all right!'

'Ridiculous,' I muttered to myself.

'I'M SITTING ON THIS CAR,' said the monster who was sitting on the roof of the car I was crouching behind.

'Yes, you are,' I agreed, but that was the end of that conversation. I mean, they were no bother, but you wouldn't want to spend much time with them. Not like you. I'm sure you're delightful company.

Slowly but surely I made my way back towards the Community Centre where El Jirafa lay waiting for me, probably wailing mournfully because she couldn't bear to be apart from me.

As I got closer to the Community Centre, I

could hear a mournful wail.

Weeeeeeeooooooowaaaaaaaaaaaaaaaaah!

It was definitely the sound of El Jirafa Tremendo wailing mournfully.

She honestly does that sometimes, if you leave her leaning against the amplifier and leave the amplifier switched on. When it happens Mum says it's 'feedback' and 'the absolute worst thing that's happened to me today', but I know it's really the sound of my guitar gently weeping.

I tried to remember if I'd switched my amp off before leaving the centre. I couldn't remember, but if I hadn't then that meant someone was messing with El Jirafa and that meant . . .

I ran the rest of the way.

Normalton Community Centre has a lot of really great features that make it perfect for band practice. It has toilets and plug sockets and Wi-Fi and a vending machine that sells pickled-onion-flavoured things.

Right now there was also loads and loads of yellow tape with black stripes wrapped round it, making it look like a birthday present for bees. The tape was emblazoned with 'Property of the Biscuit Factory – Do Not Cross' in bold, black lettering.

Other than that, everything was perfectly normal, or at least normal for today. Obviously, there were five orange monsters flapping their stupid arms at the roof of the building. The only change here was that now there was a ring of equally orange traffic cones encircling them.

WEEEEEEEOOOOOOOWAAAAAAAAAAAA AAAAAAAH! cried El Jirafa.

I walked up to the door and looked at the tape. Do not cross? Too late. I *was* cross.

I rattled the front door but it was locked.

WEEEEEEEOOOOOOOWAA—

The wailing of El Jirafa had stopped. Someone was definitely in there messing with my guitar.

'Can't you read?'

The voice came from behind me. It was cruel and nasal, like a posh anteater complaining in a hotel. It was obviously Blankley.

I spun around and there he was, with a smile like a curved trench filled with old gravestones, i.e. a bad smile.

'I just need to get in here,' I said.

'I'm afraid the Community Centre is a wholly-owned subsidiary of the Biscuit Factory.'

'What? No, it isn't. And what even is a holy-oh subway?'

'It means it belongs to us. Look, our name is on the tape.'

Flapflapflap. The tape he was talking about flapped in the breeze just to remind us what he was talking about.

'That doesn't mean you own it. You can't just slap your name on things and say they belong to you!'

'And yet, here we are.'

He folded his arms, as though saying 'here we are' had somehow won the argument.

I was about to let him know that the argument was in no way over when the door of the Community Centre rattled and opened, and out strode a seriously short man with slicked-back dirty blond hair, wearing sunglasses and a white lab coat over a garish Hawaiian shirt, which was a surprise. Even more surprising was the fact he was carrying El Jirafa Tremendo.

'Professor Whizz,' said Blankley to the short man.

'Blankley,' said the short man to Blankley.

'El Jirafa Tremendo,' I said to my guitar.

Hadz, it's truly fabooly to see you, please rescue me. This man has me by the neck, El Jirafa seemed to say.

'Did you get what you came for?' said Blankley.

The professor lifted up El Jirafa.

'This could be, like, totally the answer to everything, man,' he said.

It was certainly the answer to, 'Where's my guitar?' I thought.

'Thank you for rescuing her,' I said, holding out my hand to Professor Whizz.

He made no attempt to give my guitar back to me. He looked embarrassed.

'Ah, is this yours?' he said.

'Yes,' I said.

'No,' said Blankley.

'I beg your pardon?' I said in a very posh voice, the sort of posh voice my mum would put on if she had to phone the council to complain about the bins.

'Can't you read?' said Blankley again.

'Why do you keep asking me that?'

He smirked and pointed at El Jirafa. El Jirafa has a lot of stickers on her because I like stickers. Most of the stickers don't have words on them, just pictures of some of my favourite things. They are mostly glittery because I like glitter. And there, amongst the glittery sharks and glittery dragons and glittery skulls on glittery fire, was a yellow square with no glitter but 'Property of the Biscuit Factory' written on it in bold, black lettering.

'Did you do that? Did you put that stupid sticker on my guitar?' I asked Professor Whizz.

'No. He put that sticker on *our* guitar,' said Blankley.

83

'Oh, wow, OK, so this is awkward,' said the professor. He couldn't look me in the eye.

'Awkward? It's not awkward. You're stealing my guitar.'

'It's not yours, it's ours,' said Blankley. 'You can tell because of the sticker we've put on it.'

'You might as well say it belongs to that glittery tiger,' I said, pointing at one of the first stickers I had ever attached to El Jirafa.

'Good point. I'll tell you what, little girl,' said Blankley. 'We'll put the guitar somewhere safe and if the glittery tiger comes to claim it, then we'll pass it on for you.'

He made a sound that might have been a laugh, if there had been any sense of joy in it, but there wasn't. It was the mechanical 'ha' of a man who wouldn't recognise something genuinely funny if it had a sticker saying: 'This is genuinely funny' on it.

I turned back to Professor Whizz, who suddenly seemed to be standing on a surfboard, but that couldn't have been right.

'Please,' I said. 'You can't take El Jirafa. I need her. She's mine. Please.'

'I'll be careful with her, I promise,' said the professor.

'Careful? What, careful like you are with the fabric of the universe? You chumps at the Biscuit Factory don't know the meaning of the word "careful". You keep breaking reality! I'm not letting you break my guitar. Give it back!'

The surfboard that he was improbably standing on twitched and bucked under his feet.

'Just let me explain,' said the professor.

'There's nothing to explain,' I said. 'You people have vexed me mightily!'

'Please, I can explain if you just calm down,' said the professor.

The surfboard had started to rise into the sky. Slowly at first, and then gathering speed, the professor was flying away from me.

'Please, please calm down so we can talk about this!' said Professor Whizz.

I don't know if you've ever noticed but nobody

85

ever calmed down after somebody said 'calm down' to them. You should try it: next time somebody is having a vex, say 'calm down' to them and see what happens.

'Calm down? Come down here and say that!' I shouted, but Professor Whizz floated higher and higher.

'If you don't calm down I can't come down,' said the professor.

'I am perfectly calm!' I shouted. I don't know if you've ever noticed but nobody who ever said 'I am perfectly calm' is ever perfectly calm. In fact, I was perfectly vexed.

Somewhere in the back of my head I understood that the angrier I got, the further away Professor Whizz seemed to fly. But by heck I just wanted him and the rest of the world to know that this was not OK. This was not fine. This was a travesty!

'THIS IS A TRAVESTY!' I shouted, as Professor Whizz whooshed off.

He might have replied but by then he was too far away for me to hear.

He had flown off with El Jirafa. It was like he had stolen a part of me.

'The next bus that comes along, you'd better get on it,' said Blankley.

And lo, the sky was torn apart by lightning, and the heavens opened. Huge splattery drops of rain began to fall, and thunder shook the ground as I dropped to my knees, arms outstretched, and beseeched the gods.

'WHY!?' I cried.

That's what I felt should have happened, anyway. In reality the weather just stayed quite nice. I suppose I could have dropped to my knees and cried, 'Why!?' regardless, but Blankley was still there and I didn't want to give him the satisfaction.

Still, the universe had noticed that something dramatic definitely needed to happen at this point, so a Happybus trundled up the road and crashed right into the side of the Community Centre, which was nice.

Chapter 10

RUMRUM**KRUNCK**AKLE

Biscuits

Biscuits are a British institution, which is why we are proud to make biscuits. Pretending that everything is OK even when everything is clearly going very, very wrong is, of course, not a British institution and this is why we have nothing to do with that sort of thing.

[extracted from *Biccypedia*]

The bus had hit the Community Centre right in the side which wasn't currently being bopped by monsters. There were several noises involved.

There was the

rumrumrurm

of the bus approaching.

There was the

KERRRRUNCH!

of the bus hitting the Community Centre.

There was the

KRAAAAKAKAKAKKKAKLE

of several bricky bits of the Community Centre falling to the ground.

There was the quiet but still audible

'Ohhhhhh, for pity's sake,'

of Blankley, his head bowed and shaking, a look of severe disbelief all over his pointy face.

There was the

'Of course I didn't crash.

'Yes, everything's all right

'And no one got whiplash

'Cos everything's all right'

of somebody on the bus singing their little heart out.

And there was the

tic-tic-tic

of a little vein just under my left eye twitching at the absolute insanity of the whole situation. To be fair maybe only I could hear that bit, but honestly the whole thing was a symphony of idiocy played by an orchestra of idiots, plus my face.

Still, insanity or not, I rushed towards the bus.

'Is everyone OK?' I shouted.

Shhhhhh said the bus, adding a soft cymbal wash to the looney tunes this day was playing.

The door opened and a woman who wasn't Jill but was definitely very Jill-ish stepped out, all smiles.

She had a badge on her chest that read: 'Hi, I'm Cassie. Ask me about our Wafery Thins!'

'There were no passengers, just me. Everything's all right!' she said with a smile. 'Ouch,' she added, gingerly rubbing the back of her neck.

'Are you OK? Is your neck hurt?'

'Absolutely I'm OK,' she smiled again.

'But your neck . . .'

'How could I have hurt my neck if I didn't crash? Silly girl,' she said. 'Ouch,' she added.

'Yes, of course, silly me,' I said, with a roll of my eyes that I hoped said: 'YOU ARE COMPLETELY MENTAL BUT YOU ARE NOT MY PROBLEM.' Which I know would be *very* rude to say with your mouth but is fine to say with your eyes, I think.

I turned back to Blankley, who still had his head in his hands.

'So, am I getting on this bus?' I asked sweetly. 'Only you said I had to get on the next bus that—'

'I really can't deal with you right now,' said Blankley.

I get that a lot. But I had more to say to him.

'I dunno if you've noticed but your bus has done more damage in thirty seconds than five orange monsters did with a whole morning of flapping their ridiculous arms about.'

'Oh, I doubt that. Everything is under control,'

said Blankley. 'Everything is under control.'

Womwomwom.

His eyes didn't move from me.

'Another door has appeared, hasn't it?' he said.

I nodded, because it totally had. All floaty, and green-crackly, with a sign saying: 'Please use other door' and a monster stepping out of it.

'Everything is under control,' Blankley said.

And then he sat down and put his head between his knees and started rocking slightly.

It very much felt like the conversation was over, so I left him to it.

But I didn't go home. Did I heck. Because literally NOTHING was under control. There were buses smashing into buildings. Weird doors appearing here, there and everywhere. Stupid orange monsters lolling about being annoying. And do you know what? That was fine by me. Not my problem, mate. But worst, and most importantly, Professor Whizz had stolen my guitar. The one thing I owned that could drown out the sounds of a world gone barmy.

I realised I didn't care about the mess the Biscuit Factory had made. It wasn't going to change my plans. I was supposed to be having a band practice today and that was exactly what I was going to do.

I was going to the Biscuit Factory and I was going to steal back my guitar and nothing, NOTHING was going to stop me.

And after that I was going to find my stupid friends and drag them to the Community Centre to have a band practice, and wouldn't they be pleased that I had sorted everything out for them? And I would forgive George for getting on the bus, and Naomi for mysteriously disappearing off to wherever Naomi had mysteriously disappeared off to, and they would hug me, tears dripping from their happy, grateful faces, and thank me for being UTTERLY MOTTO and a LEGENDARILY FABOOLY FRIEND.

Yes. That's how it would go.

So I strode away from the Community Centre, and onward towards . . . MY DESTINY.

Or, more accurately, towards the bottom of Carpenter's Hill, where my epic journey into the heart of the Biscuit Factory would have to begin.

Chapter 11

GO AWAY!

Don't pANiCCCCCCC

BICcccypedia IS CURRENtly undergoing routine MAIN-
MAINMAINtenence. Please BEARWITH us as we sort
this MINOOOOOOR prolbem we probably just need to
switch the machine off AND ON again IT HAS NOTHING
TO DO WITH A OrangeMONnSTER SITTING ON THE
KEYBOOOOOAAAAAARRRRRRDDDDDDD*&^£*^%(£*")

[extracted from *Biccypedia*]

WOOOOOOOOOOO! went the siren, like a ghost
or half an owl, echoing along the tree-lined path
that led to the top of Carpenter's Hill.

The path up to the top of Carpenter's Hill is called 'Dead Man's Curvy' because it's curvy.

I think it used to be called 'Hill Walk' because you can see the words 'Hill Walk' on the little wooden sign at the bottom of the hill, but those words have been crossed out and replaced with the words 'Dead Man's Curvy' by person or persons unknown.

Around the little wooden sign there are lots of other signs with pictures of skulls and crossbones and exclamation marks and lightning bolts and little people falling off things and into things and catching fire and having things land on them.

Anyone would think that somebody didn't want people walking up this path, I thought.

I walked up the path.

YOU HAVE 1 NEW NOTIFICATION:
A MESSAGE ABOUT IGNORING SIGNS WITH
SKULLS AND LIGHTNING ON THEM

Obviously you should never, ever ignore signs with skulls and lightning on them, in case you get hit by lightning shooting out of a skull's face, or a skull with the power to shoot lightning out of its face follows you home and won't leave you alone and makes teatime really awkward as it flies round the kitchen zapping things with its face-lightning while you try to tell your mum that you totally didn't even see the signs warning you that this was exactly what would happen.

Having said all that, if you ever find yourself in the situation where a Super-Secret Science Lab is throwing big orange monsters about the place, and they've stolen your guitar, and the only way to get it back is to ignore a bunch of signs with skulls and lightning on them . . .

I trust you to use your own judgement.

A bit further up the path was a sign that read:

And underneath the writing was a picture of a skull with lightning coming out of it. The skull had a speech bubble which said:

I ignored it and
kept walking.

A bit further up the path was a sign that read:

WE CAN'T HELP BUT NOTICE YOU IGNORED THE LAST SIGN. JUST SO YOU KNOW, IF YOU GO ANY FURTHER WE'RE PROBABLY ALLOWED TO SHOOT YOU.

I was pretty sure they probably weren't allowed to shoot me. You can't just go around shooting people walking up a path. That must be a rule, I thought.

I kept walking.

A bit further up the path was a sign that read:

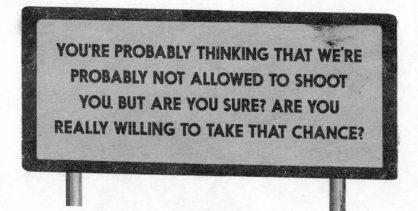

YOU'RE PROBABLY THINKING THAT WE'RE PROBABLY NOT ALLOWED TO SHOOT YOU. BUT ARE YOU SURE? ARE YOU REALLY WILLING TO TAKE THAT CHANCE?

I kept walking.

A bit further up the path was a sign that read:

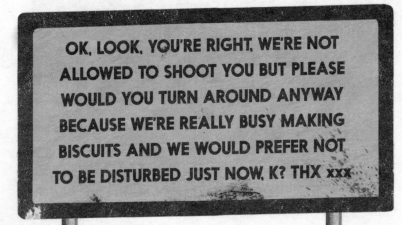

OK, LOOK, YOU'RE RIGHT, WE'RE NOT
ALLOWED TO SHOOT YOU BUT PLEASE
WOULD YOU TURN AROUND ANYWAY
BECAUSE WE'RE REALLY BUSY MAKING
BISCUITS AND WE WOULD PREFER NOT
TO BE DISTURBED JUST NOW, K? THX xxx

And so on and so on. It took about half an hour to walk up the hill, and I passed a new sign every two minutes or so, alternately pleading, threatening, and in one case, baffling:

RABBITS
IN YOUR FACE.
CAUTION

I kept walking, thinking my thoughts about orange monsters and Happybuses and band practice and wishing I had George or even Naomi with me so I could share my thoughts, and then we would laugh, and then they would say something funny, and we would laugh again and it would be nicer than walking alone.

I had been through times of having no friends before and I got through them, but having real friends was better.

But then real friends wouldn't have let me down so badly. George was happily sitting on a bus, and Naomi was . . .

I suddenly remembered I still had no idea where the heck Naomi was, but then in many ways she was a mystery to me.

I tried to picture her face, but even that was a bit . . . fuzzy.

She was basically a collection of amazing clothes, accessories and attitude.

I missed her. Just standing next to her made me feel cooler than I was.

And just standing next to George made me feel braver.

And here I was. Alone. Uncool. And a little bit scared.

They had abandoned me. In many ways it was their fault I was lonely and frightened in a deep dark wood.

But I missed them anyway. Life is complicated and no mistake. If life was a dance routine you'd need at least seven legs and double-jointed elbows to do all the moves properly.

At the top of Dead Man's Curvy the path emerged from the trees, and there squatting on top of the hill was the Biscuit Factory. It was a long, rectangular building, two storeys high, made of red bricks which said, 'This is a perfectly normal building,' and massive tinted windows which said, 'We totally have something to hide.' It was surrounded by tall wire fencing with spikes on the top which agreed with what the windows were saying, i.e. 'There is no way we are just making biscuits in here'.

Men and women in Biscuit Factory overalls ran back and forth around the building, shouting into phones and walkie-talkies and each other's faces things like:

'I need a sitrep, stat!'

And:

'This is a Code Seven Cataclysm! Repeat, Code Seven!'

And:

'We are through the looking glass here, people!'

All the stuff that people in uniform like to shout when things go a bit crisis-shaped. I wasn't sure any of it meant anything, but hopefully it was making them all feel better.

'We have another ABC incursion!' shouted a man in beige Biscuit Factory overalls into his wrist.

He was standing just by the gate, which was open to allow vans with 'Mmmm, Biscuits!' written on the side to drive in and out. I walked over to him.

On his chest was a badge saying: 'Hi, I'm

Trevor. Ask me about our Nibbly NomNoms!'

'Hi, Trevor,' I said to him. 'How are your Nibbly NomNoms?'

'What?'

Small talk over, I went in for the kill. I had thought about various ruses to try and get into the factory, but I'd had my fill of ridiculous lies this morning, so I decided to try the one strategy I figured the Biscuit Factory would be unable to deal with: the truth.

'So hey, that's great about the Nibbly NomNoms,' I said. 'I'm here for my guitar.'

'You're what?' he said.

'A short man on a flying surfboard stole my guitar and I think he brought it here, so I'm here to get it. Is that OK?'

'Is it OK?' said Trevor. 'Everything's gone to heck and nobody knows where the Chief is. Basically, we've got ourselves a Code Seven Cataclysm here. Absolutely nothing is OK, do you understand?'

'No,' I said sweetly and I fluttered my eyelashes

at him, which, by the way, is really hard to do if you're not a cartoon. I may have looked adorably adorable, or I may have looked like I was having a seizure. The man didn't seem to care either way.

'A Code Seven Cataclysm is the absolute worst . . . wait a minute, do you work here? You're from the town, aren't you?'

He didn't give me time to answer.

'Oh, well, ahem,' he continued. 'A Code Seven Cataclysm is . . . fine. It just means everything's fine and dandy. No problems at all.'

He smiled a not-terribly-convincing smile at me.

'Oh, super-duper!' I said. 'So if everything is fine I can get my guitar then?'

He stared at me. There was something about his expression that made me think he was wishing he was allowed to shoot me.

'I can't deal with you right now,' he said. 'Why don't you . . . why don't you go to reception?' he said, pointing through the gate to a door in the side of the building. 'Go tell Maureen that you want your guitar, see where that gets you.'

There was a **womwomwom** and another floating door with lime-green crackles and a sign saying: 'Please use other door' appeared to our left.

There was a **womwomwom** and another floating door with lime-green crackles and a sign saying: 'Please use other door' appeared to our right.

'Event intensity escalating!' he shouted. 'People, this is—'

He caught my eye and coughed slightly.

'Fine! Absolutely normal, nothing to worry about,' he added. Lowering his voice, he hissed at me, 'Go see Maureen,' and then he ran off somewhere really quickly, like people do when there's absolutely nothing to worry about.

So I walked in through the gate. I was just heading for reception when a rabbit launched itself at my face, which was really all my own fault because I had ignored the warning signs.

Chapter 12

FLUMPH

FILE NOT FOUND

Sorry we cannot find the page you are looking for.
Have you tried looking under THE BIG HECKIN'
MONSTER? ←----- who wrote this? See me!

[extracted from *Biccypedia*]

'Don't I know you?' I said to the rabbit.

The rabbit didn't answer, probably because it was busy flying towards my face at high speed like a white, fluffy bullet. I tried to duck but it was moving too fast. Before I knew it, FLUMPH! I had a face full of rabbit.

I wasn't 100 per cent sure I recognised it. I thought it might have been the rabbit from my garden that morning. It was definitely wearing the same bright red boots. But on the other hand, it was wearing large, square, thick-rimmed glasses, so it was hard to be sure. Especially now it was very, very close to my face. Too close, really. The rabbit was clinging to my head and was showing no signs of letting go.

I grabbed it and tried to pull it off me but it was too strong.

'Get off me!' I cried, or at least I tried to. It sounded more like, 'Gt mff muh,' because I had a face full of rabbit.

'I'm sorry. I was doing a mighty leap and your face got in the way. Do you need help?' said the rabbit.

'Pls gt mff muh,' I said.

'I am here to help you,' said the rabbit.

'Pls. Gt. Mff. Muh. Fsh,' I said, as slowly and clearly as I could.

The rabbit dropped off my face and stood in front of me on its hind legs, whiskers twitching.

'My name is Man Man,' said the rabbit. 'I am a man.'

Its eyes were bright red and sparkly, like a pair of rubies in the snow.

'My name is Haddie,' I said. 'I am a . . . wait a minute, you do know you're a rabbit, don't you?'

'Haha,' said Man Man. 'Of course I'm not a rabbit. Look.' And he tapped his glasses. 'I'm wearing glasses which, if you think about it, is exactly what a rabbit wouldn't do. Do you need help?'

'I think one of us does, definitely.'

'I am Man Man,' said the rabbit. 'I am a superhero. I have all the powers and abilities of a man, and I am a man, hence the name.'

'Right,' I said. 'Right. Good. That's all great. Did I see you in my garden this morning? I saw a rabbit about your size, only without the glasses.'

'This so-called rabbit you saw, was he vanquishing foes?'

109

'Yes, there was definitely some vanquishing going on,' I said, remembering the pile of bruised Biscuitrons I had walked past.

'Well, I mean, it sounds a bit like me. I *do* do a lot of vanquishing. It's kind of my thing. But I am a man, and definitely not a rabbit. You probably got confused, perhaps because I had forgotten to put my Man-glasses on. Those foes were trying to drag me into a van to take me back to the Factory,' he said, jerking a paw towards the Biscuit Factory.

'You're from the Factory?'

'No, I'm from another dimension. I got sucked into this dimension, without so much as a, "Would you mind awfully being transported through a glowing portal into a world very different from your own?" They dragged us here, then the portal closed and they couldn't get it open again. So while they were faffing about with the portal we escaped and that is my origin story.'

I was just about to ask him about the words 'we' and 'us', but the chatty little maniac kept talking and I forgot about it for a while, secure in the belief that that words 'we' and 'us' would in no way be important to the story later.

'So . . . do you need help?' said Man Man. 'I can help. I am Man Man. This is kind of my first day as a superhero and I could really do with finding someone to help.'

He stood with his fuzzy little legs quite far apart and put his paws on his hips. He did look pretty heroic, I have to say. And maybe having a superhero along for the ride would be a good thing.

'OK, Man Man, I do need your help. They've taken El Jirafa Tremendo, and I think she's in there.' I gestured at the main building. 'Being experimented on.'

'A rescue mission! Hot dog! We will rescue your giraffe,' said Man Man. 'We are having a team-up, like the Avengers or the Justice League.'

'Or *Watership Down*,' I added helpfully.

'If you say so! Let us go and commit mighty deeds!'

'Hey, you!'

The voice was cruel and nasal, like a hungry crocodile with a cork up each nostril. It was coming from behind me.

I didn't need to turn round to know that it was Blankley but I turned round anyway.

'What do you think you're doing?' he said.

'I'm teaming up with this superhero to rescue El Jirafa from that Super-Secret Science Lab,' I recapped beautifully for anybody who wasn't 100 per cent sure what was going on. 'Why, what are you doing? Nice to see you up and about. I take it kneeling on the floor rocking and crying didn't work out for you?'

'I wasn't crying,' snapped Blankley. 'And you can't prove I was.'

'Who is this?' asked Man Man.

'He works here,' I said. 'I think his job is not coping with things very well. He's good at it. He helped steal El Jirafa.'

'Oh, is that a fact?' said Man Man. 'I think I need to have words with this man, man to man.'

'What? No, let's just run,' I said, but it was too late, Man Man was already striding up to Blankley.

'Run? I don't think so. Running is what a . . . a . . . a rabbit would do. And I,' said Man Man, 'am a man. You there, where is this girl's giraffe?'

He had reached Blankley and was looking up at him.

'I'll ask the questions,' said Blankley.

'Ask *this*!' said Man Man, which didn't really make any sense, but nobody had a chance to tell him that because he immediately launched himself at Blankley.

BAMBAMBAMBAMBAMBAMBAM

There was a white, bristly blur of kicks and punches, then Blankley crumpled slowly to the ground as Man Man put his paws back to his hips and stared into the distance with one rabbit eyebrow raised. He did look heroic.

'Wherever evil shall be fought, Man Man will . . . uh, something ought. Bought. Taut. Plort. Heckit,' said Man Man. 'I'm trying to come up with a rhyme to say after vanquishing a foe. It's quite hard.'

Blankley said nothing. He just lay on the ground, unconscious.

'Oh heck, Man Man! You shouldn't have done that.'

'I am afraid I had to,' said Man Man. 'It is my duty as Man Man to use the powers of a man to fight men with my man fists. With great power comes a lot of mighty punching and what-have-you. It's a man thing.' He looked off into the distance again, his fuzzy rabbit face carrying an expression that was either deeply thoughtful or the look of someone trying to hold in a fart.

'I'm sorry, Man Man, but you can't just go around battering everyone who vexes you. It's wrong and bad, and also it would take too long because there's a lot of vexy people around these days and we've got things to do. Also, you knocked him out and now he can't tell us where El Jirafa is.'

'Ah. Yes, well, OK. Perhaps I was a little too mighty. I am just getting used to my man powers.

Next time I will be more careful.'

'Right. Good,' I said. 'Come on then. Let's go—
Woah my heck, have you farted?'

Which was not how that last sentence was
supposed to end, but an invisible catastrophe
had just invaded my nostrils. It smelled like
some broccoli had died up my nose.

'Yes, I have,' said Man Man proudly. 'It's what
men do. And I am . . . Man Man!'

We headed for reception.

Chapter 13

TAP TAP TAP

CLOSED FOR
MAINTENANCE

Biccypedia is currently closed for routine maintenance.
Please come back in, oh, hopefully around 16 chapters
should do it.

[extracted from *Biccypedia*]

The reception area was like every reception area
you've ever seen. It was a clean, bright box for
keeping a person in. It was bathed in fluorescent
lighting and decorated with a large potted plant.

In the corner was the person who was kept there: Maureen.

Maureen looked like a Monday morning in a white blouse. Like a deep sigh on a swivel chair. Like getting socks for Christmas, in human form.

Maureen was very visibly a disappointed human being.

Maureen was sitting behind a desk with a telephone, a computer and a little sign with 'Maureen' written on it. Pinned to her blouse was a badge with: 'Hi, I'm Maureen. Ask me about our Crumbly Oaties!' written on it. The phone rang.

'Hello, Maureen speaking,' she said. 'Putting you through.'

'Hello,' I said. 'Are you Maureen?' because even in highly tense infiltration situations, I am funny.

WOAH YEAH!

Maureen sighed as she put down the phone.

'Welcome to the Biscuit Factory, how may I be of assistance?' she said to the computer's screen. I assumed she was talking to the screen because

117

that's where she was looking, as she tapped a single key on the keyboard with a puzzled expression on her face.

Tap tap tap.

To one side were three doors. Two were toilets and one was marked: 'No Entrance'. I guessed that was the one we wanted.

'I'm here for my guitar,' I said.

She didn't look up from the computer.

'Nobody told me about a guitar,' said Maureen. 'Typical.'

Tap tap.

'Oh, OK,' I said. 'So can I go and get it?'

'Nobody tells me anything round here,' said Maureen. 'There could be a Code Seven Cataclysm happening out there right now and I wouldn't know about it because nobody tells me anything round here.'

'Well, yeah, so . . . are you going to let me in?' I said.

'Why would I?'

Tap tap.

'Because I need to get my guitar.'

'I don't know anything about a guitar.'

'I know, because nobody tells you anything round here.'

'Tell me about it.'

Tap.

'But I am, you see, I am telling you about it! That's what is happening right now. Somebody is telling you something.'

Her finger paused over whichever key she had been tapping and she finally looked up at me.

'Telling me about what?' she said.

'About the guitar!'

She tutted.

'Guitar? There's a guitar now, is there? Typical,' she said. 'Nobody tells me anything round here.'

And she went back to looking at the screen and tapping.

Tap tap tap.

I was beginning to get vexy. I looked down to share a look with Man Man but he wasn't there. Where had he gone? I looked round the reception area but there was no sign of him. There was also no sign of the large potted plant that had been just inside the front entrance.

I looked up. Man Man was hanging off one of the fluorescent strip lights by his feet, directly above Maureen. He was upside down and grasping the large potted plant between his paws. He gave me a wink.

'Don't!' I said, as I gestured at Man Man to get down from the ceiling.

'Don't what?' said Maureen.

Tap tap tap.

'Don't . . . uh, don't you know you're on fire?' I said to her. I didn't really know what I was saying, just that I had to get her out of that swivel chair before Man Man dropped a plant pot on her.

'Am I? Typical. Nobody tells me anything round here,' she said. She didn't look away from the monitor.

'Yeah, your foot is totally on fire. You should probably get some water, to stop the fire from spreading.'

'Is that how you stop fire, is it? With water? Typical. Nobody tells me anything round here.'

'You should go to the bathroom, where there's taps, with water in them.'

'There's a bathroom in here? With taps? With water in them?' said Maureen.

'I know. *Typical*,' I said. 'I'll look after the desk for you.'

She looked up at me again.

'And who are you?' She peered at me, her expression never altering from the slightly pained look of confusion that she was obviously stuck with.

'I don't know. Nobody told me.'

'Typical,' said Maureen.

'Typical,' I agreed.

She pointed at a button on her desk.

'That opens the door,' she said. 'Don't let anybody in unless someone tells you to, which they won't because . . .'

'Nobody tells you anything round here,' I finished her sentence for her.

And with that Maureen got up from her swivel chair and moped over to the bathroom.

'What the heck were you thinking?' I said to Man Man as he nimbly dropped from the ceiling without dropping so much as a speck of soil from the potted plant.

'I was thinking of dropping this big plant on her head,' he said. 'Is that not what it looked like I was thinking?'

'Well, think again. You see how I dealt with the situation, and nobody had to get hurt.'

'I saw. I liked your style. We are having a classic team-up!' said Man Man. 'That's what we superheroes do. We have a team-up and use our different powers to vanquish foes. You certainly fooled her! Haha, she won't be happy when she finds out she's not on fire.'

I looked over at the bathroom door.

'You're probably right,' I said.

'Maybe I should quickly pop in there and deliver a mighty blow with this just to be on the safe side,' said Man Man, lifting up the potted plant with a hopeful smile. 'Do a proper vanquishing.'

'You could but then somebody would have to tell her fifteen times that she was supposed to fall over. Waste of time,' I said. 'Come on, let's get going.'

I hit the door release button, and the door marked 'No Entrance' swung open with a *kerchik*, magically becoming an entrance.

Chapter 14

CLACK CLACK CLACK

The door *ker-chakk*ed closed behind us. We were in a corridor, long and well-lit and empty. There were doors coming off it at regular intervals on each side. I walked to the first door, which was marked: **Interdimensional Management**.

The next one was marked: **Realms (misc.)**.

The next one was marked: **Infinity (and Beyond)**.

All the stuff you'd expect in a Biscuit Factory that wasn't actually a Biscuit Factory at all.

Where would they be keeping El Jirafa? This was going to take ages.

I ran further down the corridor. The next door was marked: **Biscuit**.

Which was weird because why would there be any biscuits in the Biscuit Factory? The Biscuit Factory was the last place you'd expect to find any biscuits.

'Come on, keep moving,' said Man Man. He was panting slightly because he was still dragging the potted plant with him.

'What did you bring that for?' I said.

'In case of foes.'

'There's nobody about, Man Man,' I said. 'You might as well put it d—'

Ker-chik.

That was the No Entry door opening again!

I grabbed Man Man by the ears and dragged him and his stupid plant pot into the Biscuit room and closed the door.

We were in a large, square, windowless room. At its centre was a battered metal filing cabinet with three drawers. The middle drawer was marked with the letter 'b' and locked shut with a padlock.

'Why are we hiding? There's only . . .' his ears twitched madly '. . . two . . . no, three of them!' said Man Man. 'Let me go out there and rough them up a little.'

'Shush,' I said.

'Also, these,' he said, pointing at his ears, 'are extremely sensitive auditory instruments. They are NOT a carry-handle!'

'OK, sorry. You do have quite big ears, though. For a man, I mean.'

'You have quite a big mouth. For a girl, I mean,' said Man Man sniffily.

I decided not to mention he also had a very small, pink nose for a man. It was mesmerising, twitching up and down. It really was twitching a lot.

'Oh my,' he said, sniffing the air. 'Do you smell that? There is something delicious in here. Are you hungry? I'm hungry.'

He padded towards the filing cabinet.

I needed to be sure that whoever had entered

the corridor hadn't seen us. Pressing my ear against the door, I could hear the *clack clack clack* of their shoes on the corridor as they moved towards our room.

Clack clack clack went their footsteps, and then of course, OF COURSE, they stopped right outside the door.

I froze, unsure of what to do if they came in, but the door stayed shut.

And then they started talking, their voices muffled by the door.

'Good news, we've come up with a name for them – ABCs. Stands for Annoying Big Creatures.'

This voice was cruel and nasal, like a sarky aardvark. Blankley.

'Oh hey, great name. Love it, man.' I recognised the lazy drawl of Professor Whizz. 'Names are totes important. People take me a whole lot more seriously since I changed my first name to "Professor", anyway. And have you, like, worked out how we're going to deal with these ABCs?

Because I have a couple of ideas.'

There was a longish silence. I turned to see Man Man cautiously approaching the filing cabinet in the middle of the room, his adorable pink nose twitching away.

'Oh, there is something tasty in here,' he whispered.

Meanwhile, the Biscuitrons in the corridor had started talking again.

'I think the main problem is . . . well, as you all know we have a Department for Opening Doors in Reality.' This was a new voice, quieter and more hesitant than the other two, the sort of voice you'd imagine coming from a small hedgehog or a medium-sized vole, and the way today was going, it might well have been either.

'Great department!' said Whizz. 'And super-successful – we've opened so many doors in reality! Thankfully most of them close more or less of their own accord.'

'Yes, and I think that's a credit to us,' said the

hedgehog-or-vole. 'The only slight issue is, and I'm sure it won't prove to be too much of a problem, but I do feel it's worth noting, although actually in many ways it's more of an opportunity than a problem when you think about it, but . . .'

'Stan? Hate to rush you but is there any chance that this sentence might get to a point?' said Blankley.

'Oh, right, yes, so the thing is, we don't seem to have a Department for Closing Doors in Reality,' said Stan-the-maybe-vole.

'Really? I doubt that. Have you checked?'

'So, I asked Maureen and she says nobody has told her about any such department.'

'Hardly conclusive.'

'I know but, you see, I had a quick look on Biccypedia and there's no mention of a Department for Closing Doors in Reality in there, either.'

'Frankly, I doubt that's true,' said Blankley. 'If, as Whizz says, the doors usually close on their own anyway, that probably means the Department for Closing Doors in Reality are sitting in a room somewhere, taking selfies and playing Candy Crush, just waiting for the call to swing into action.'

'But . . .'

'Seriously, Stan, think about it. It would be utterly ridiculous for a Super-Secret Science Lab to have a Department for Opening Doors in Reality, if there wasn't a Department for Closing Doors in Reality! I mean, that would be reckless! It would be dangerous! It would be . . . it would be . . .'

'Um . . . unthinkable?'

'Unthinkable! Yes! So let's not think about it. I simply refuse to think that there is no Department for Closing Holes in Reality. And instead I choose to think that there IS one and that they are working hard even as we speak to close this OneWay Wild Wandering WayDoor that our department has so successfully opened between our reality and whatever weird dimension these

ABCs are tumbling out of.'

OneWay Wild Wandering WayDoor, I thought. Presumably he was talking about the double doors with the green crackles that were causing all the trouble around town.

'I totally think I know how to close this door, man,' said Whizz.

'Good grief, are you not listening? It's simply not our responsibility, as the Department for Opening Holes in Reality, to be going around worrying about how we close those holes in reality. It's clearly the responsibility of the Department for *Closing* Holes in Reality. Which, as we have discussed, simply must exist, whether we know about it or not. So that's it. We'll just continue coning and taping off the ABCs and wait for everything to get sorted out.'

'I think the guitar might be the key to sorting all this out,' said Whizz.

WOAH YEAH!

What the hey? Simmer down, choir of angels. You're only supposed to sing when it's *me* who says something amazing.

'I don't think I've made myself clear,' said Blankley. 'Sorting this out is not our responsibility, and if I find anyone in this department even so much as *trying* to sort this out there'll be trouble! How does that sound?'

'Dude, that sounds . . . amazing,' said Whizz. 'I mean, I'm amazed you said it. So . . . amazing. Yeah.'

My goodness me. El Jirafa Tremendo could be the key to sorting out this whole problem. This news was . . .

Interesting.

Irritating.

Deeply, deeply vexing.

Because I wanted my guitar back.

Because I wanted to play her right now.

This complicated matters.

We would have to move fast.

Clack clack clack.

They had started to walk away from the door, their voices getting more distant as they walked.

'Um, so I suppose someone should tell the Chief? So, has anyone seen the Chief recently?'

'He must be around somewhere.'

'Of course he must. He wouldn't just run away and hide at this time of crisis, that would be . . . I mean that would be . . .'

'Unthinkable?'

'Yes, exactly, so let's not think it!'

'Um . . . OK, I suppose . . .'

This was a lot to take in. I needed some time to think about what I had heard, so obviously this was the precise moment that Man Man chose to pick a fight with the filing cabinet in the middle of the room, and someone opened the door.

He was wearing Biscuit Factory overalls and a badge which read: 'Hi, I'm Stan! Ask me about our Quinoa Clumps!'

'What the absolute heck is going on here?' he said.

I sighed.

'Right now,' I said, 'your guess is as good as mine.'

Chapter 15

KLANG KLANG KLANG

Basically what was happening in here was I was looking into Stan's confused face while behind me Man Man was whacking the filing cabinet over and over again with a large potted plant.

KLANG KLANG KLANG.

So what else could I say?

'I am an eleven-year-old girl who has just successfully broken in to a Super-Secret Science Lab, and this rabbit,' and here I gestured at Man Man, 'and this rabbit is . . . actually, Man Man, what are you doing?'

Man Man paused, huffing and puffing.

'I am mightily vanquishing this metal box with a large potted plant.'

And then he started hitting the cabinet again, swinging the potted plant with gusto.

KLANG KLANG KLANG.

'Also I'm not a rabbit, I am Man Man.'

'Oh yes. He's a superhero, and he's mightily vanquishing that cabinet with a plant pot.'

Stan stood in silence for a moment. His left eye twitched. He opened his mouth as if he was about to say something, but no words came out. His left eye twitched again.

And then he slowly closed the door and we never saw Stan again. Some people just aren't cut out for working in a Super-Secret Science Lab, I thought. And I never even had a chance to ask him about his Quinoa Clumps.

There was a sudden *KLATTER* behind me.

I turned to see a broken padlock spinning across the floor, and the middle drawer of the cabinet hanging open.

Man Man was staring into the open drawer. His eyes had glazed over and he was drooling.

'Oh my,' he said. 'It's . . . it's beautiful.'

Whatever was in there was lighting his face with a faint golden glow.

'What, what's beautiful?' I trotted over and took a look into the drawer marked 'B'.

'Oh, of course,' I said. 'B for biscuit.'

There at the bottom of the drawer was a perfectly round, perfectly baked cookie that shone with the golden light of late summer evenings.

'Do you think they made this here?' I whispered.

'You'll have to speak up,' said Man Man. 'I can't hear you over how delicious this biscuit smells.'

I reached into the drawer and picked it up.

'Halvsies?' I said and broke the biscuit in two. Oh my. Just snapping it was a treat for the senses. Crisp and crumbly around the edge and slightly gooey in the centre, the two pieces separating with an almost audible sigh.

I handed Man Man half, and then brought my half to my nose. It smelled of childhood afternoons, of crackling winter fires, of flour and butter and sugar. It smelled of love, twice baked.

It smelled like a really, really nice biscuit.

And then I put it in my mouth, and I felt like I slipped into a bath of warm honey, no, I felt like the bath slipped into me. I felt warm. I felt happy. I felt content.

'That was a tasty biscuit,' said Man Man.

'What?' I said, looking over at him. He was blurry, because my eyes were prickling with tears, tears for the fact I might never taste such sun-dappled crumbly sweetness again.

'This place is crazy,' I said. 'They can make biscuits like that and instead they choose to break holes in the fabric of reality and plop big, daft Bumblefluffs all over town. That biscuit was . . . I mean, it was totally . . . I mean, wow, you know?'

'Oh, I know. It was . . . yeah. Wow.'

We might have stayed there for days, smacking our lips, recalling flavours and sensations that were impossible to put into words other than 'wow', if a sudden scream outside the door hadn't snapped us out of it.

Chapter 16

BWAAAAR WAAARM CHIKKA CHIKKA BWARM BU-BU-BWARM BWAR

WEEEE-AARRRR-WOOOOO.

'Hark!' said Man Man. 'There is trouble afoot!' and he burst out of the Biscuit room into the corridor, with me following close behind.

'Somebody is getting hurt down there,' said Man Man.

We moved further down the corridor. The scream came again.

WEEEE-ARRRR-WOOOO BWAAAAR WAAARM CHIKKA CHIKKA BU-BU-BWARM BWAR.

'That's not the sound of someone in pain, you plum! That's someone playing guitar.'

'Really?' said Man Man, his ears swivelling back and forth. 'I can't honestly tell the difference.'

I ran down the corridor, following the sound of riffing and soloing. Finally I came to a door marked R&D&D&D. The noises were definitely coming from in there.

The door had a frosted glass panel in it. I could sort of see someone moving around in there but the frosting meant I couldn't tell exactly what was going on.

Man Man caught up with me, huffing and puffing, still carrying the battered remains of his potted plant.

'I think El Jirafa's in here,' I said. 'We need a plan.'

'Wherever evil seeks to hide, that's when door and pot collide!' he said and he threw the potted plant through the frosted pane of glass, which shattered noisily, bits of glass and wood flying everywhere.

After the noise came silence, broken only by the occasional tinkling of small bits of glass dropping away from what was left of the window frame.

'What did you do that for? There's a door handle,' I said, exasperated.

'I am . . . Man Man!' said Man Man and he jumped through the empty window frame.

'That's not an actual reason!' I shouted after him, but it was pointless arguing with the hairy little hooligan.

I sighed and opened the door. The broken glass under my feet scrunched and popped as I walked in to the R&D&D&D room.

There was a bunch of stuff to see in there. It was like a mad scientist's dream, with computer monitors flashing, test tubes bubbling, whizzy things whizzing, spinny things spinning, bleepy things bleeping, and metal boxes whirring and humming. There was an awful lot to see, but my thoughts were interrupted by a coughing, gurgling sound. I tore my eyes away from the technoclutter and focused on what was

141

happening in front of it.

Professor Whizz was sprawled on the floor. He had El Jirafa Tremendo still strapped to him and on top of the guitar stood Man Man, one foot on the fretboard and one foot on the professor's neck.

The gurgling noise was coming from the professor.

'Take that, vile criminal! Now where is this girl's giraffe?' shouted Man Man.

Professor Whizz just gurgled in reply.

'Man Man! What the heck do you think you're doing? Get off him right now!'

Man Man looked over at me, shaking his head in bafflement.

'What? What am I doing wrong now?'

'You're standing on his neck. How's he supposed to answer your question when you're standing on his neck?'

Man Man glared at me for a moment.

'That . . .' he said. 'That is actually a fair point. Hot cakes! I have to say being a superhero is a lot more complicated than I thought it would be.'

He took his foot off the professor's windpipe.

The professor coughed and sputtered.

'Woah, dude, this is turning into a day of amazing new experiences,' he said. 'Choked by a rabbit. Wow. Extreme. Thanks, man.'

He smiled at Man Man. Clearly the professor was the kind of person who tries to see the best in every situation.

'I am not a rabbit, I am a man,' said Man Man.

'Oh right, of course you are. I didn't see the glasses. Sorry, man.'

'Man Man.'

'Sorry, Man Man.'

'Man Man,' I said. 'Will you get the heck off El Jirafa? You'll damage her.'

'This is your giraffe, Haddie?' said Man Man, looking down at the professor. 'Hello. I thought you'd be taller.'

'He's not the giraffe. There is no giraffe. My guitar is called El Jirafa Tremendo.'

'Why?'

'Because that's her name.'

He stepped off the guitar and Professor Whizz got himself back to his feet.

'Haddie, Man Man, super-great to meet you! Hey! Guess what? I don't want to make too big a deal out of this but if I can't work out how to play this thing properly the world is probably, like, really probably going to end quite soon. Like, sooner than you'd want, anyway. Like, in three hours, which is quite soon, isn't it? Like, it would be a long time to wait for a train, but not for the end of the world, know what I mean?'

'Sorry, what?'

YOU HAVE 1 NEW NOTIFICATION:
A MESSAGE ABOUT SUSPENSE

'The world will really probably end quite soon.' Yikes, right? What I have done there is 'good storytelling' because I have created suspense but actually I feel like I need to tell you that the world is going to be OK. I mean,

kind of OK. Mostly OK. As OK as you can be when you're three hours away from ending, which is . . . you know, not ideal.

What I mean is, if you had just been told the world was going to end in three hours I probably wouldn't bother asking, 'Are you OK?' because you'd be unlikely to reply: 'No worries! I'm golden! A scientist just told me the world's about to end, that's all!'

'Are you OK?' would be a silly question in those circumstances.

But I really want you to know everything is going to be OK because at this point I didn't know it was going to be OK and that felt really, truly awful, probably the worst I've ever felt and I don't want you to feel like that so I'll say again: it's going to be OK. Sort of. Mostly OK.

U OK?

OK. On to the next bit.

'Are you OK?' said Whizz, who clearly hadn't read the notification about suspense.

'So . . . how long have we got, exactly?' I asked.

The professor grabbed a tablet from a work surface beside him and started tapping at it.

'OK, so there's good news and bad news. The sciPad says we only have three hours to save the world,' he said.

'Oh,' I said. 'Oh no. What's the good news?'

'That *was* the good news. The bad news is we only have a 0.35 chance of success which is . . . well, I suppose it's better than a 0.34 chance, isn't it?'

'The world is going to end?' I said.

'To be fair that's only around a 99.65 per cent probability.'

I didn't know what to say. This was terrible news.

'The world is in peril?' said Man Man with a huge grin. 'Hot sauce! That's brilliant news! High five, everyone!'

Chapter 17

KABLOOEY

Man Man was grinning and holding up his paw for someone, anyone to lay five on it, but I was stunned.

Three hours? How can anybody save the world in three hours? One hundred and eighty minutes? Around ten chapters?

I can barely brush my hair adequately in three hours.

I sat down and stared into space. It seemed pointless doing anything else.

Man Man sat next to me.

'Hey,' he said. 'Don't be sad. We can sort this

out! All I need to do is punch some foes in the face and everything will be right as rain. It's just a matter of working out who to punch. Hot mail! This is like a dream come true!'

'Please, Man Man, I'm trying to be despondent here.'

'Although I suppose I could just punch *everyone*,' he continued. 'Then at least I'd be guaranteed to be punching the right person eventually.'

'It's easy for you, you're a superhero. You're used to saving the world.'

'I'll let you into a little secret,' said Man Man. 'Promise you won't tell anyone?'

I nodded.

He took his glasses off.

'I'm not actually a man at all. I'm a rabbit. The glasses are a disguise. And here's another secret. The glasses don't give me the power of a man. I put these on and I pretend to have the power of a man. And it seems to work.'

'It's . . . a good disguise,' I lied.

'Holy Hawking, where did Man Man go?' said the professor. 'And where did this relatively tall rabbit come from?'

Maybe I was wrong about the disguise.

'Small scientist, I have to tell you something that may surprise you,' said Man Man and as he explained himself to the professor I had a word with myself.

I did not want the world to end. Not one bit. Of course, the world was vexy and confusing and weird, but it was my home and my friends lived here.

My friends! Oh heck, where were my friends? Sitting somewhere, totally unaware of the danger they were in. I envied them, a bit. Wouldn't I rather be sitting somewhere, happily ignorant of the fate of the world?

And my mum! Sitting quietly at home, trying not to be a bother to anyone, getting stressed if she had to leave the house. If she was lucky she wouldn't notice the world ending.

Maybe I could just go home and pretend

everything was all right, like everybody else in this stupid town.

Maybe someone else would sort this problem out.

My friends had abandoned me and my mum was a bit weird but they were all I had, apart from my guitar, but what use is a guitar without friends to enjoy it with and a mum to get annoyed by it?

Yeah. So, no.

No, I wasn't going to ignore it.

Yeah, I was going to do something.

I resolved there and then to do my best to save this stupid planet, and if that meant postponing band practice for a day or two then so be it. I'm fairly sure you would have done the same.

'So you're, like, a proper superhero?' the professor was saying. 'Epic!'

I stood up.

'I have an announcement to make,' I said. 'Band practice is cancelled!'

WOAH YEAH!

'Er, OK,' said Whizz.

'Hot jacket potatoes!' said Man Man. 'What's a band practice?'

'Let's just get back on topic,' I said. 'The end of the world? How did this happen? It's only a few Bumblefluffs . . . or what did Blankley call them . . . ABCs! And they're not exactly dangerous, just annoying. How come we suddenly only have three hours to save the world?'

'OK, here's the deal,' said Professor Whizz. 'If my calculations are correct, and of course they are, then . . . OK, let's think of a metaphor. Can you imagine a tap, only instead of water, there are large, annoying, orange creatures pouring out of it? And imagine the world is a sink. Like, a really big sink. Can you picture that?'

'Of course I can, but how does that help?'

'Good point. OK, scratch that. Instead, can you picture a tear in the fabric of reality, a door between dimensions. And can you imagine creatures from one dimension are being inexorably drawn into our dimension? That's a much better metaphor, because it's what is actually happening.'

'I don't think that's how metaphors work.'

'Well, they should. It really takes the guesswork out of it if you actually describe what is happening. And what is actually happening here is that in three hours the amount of extra-dimensional stuff coming into our dimension will be so great that even if we *can* work out how to shut the door, which currently we can't, we won't be able to do it. The door will stick open, and then other bits of their dimension will start coming through.'

'Other bits? What other bits?'

'Well, all of it. Plants, rocks, frisbees, if indeed there are frisbees in other dimensions – my research so far has been inconclusive – also moons, planets . . . our dimension will get flooded by this other dimension and then both dimensions will be trying to occupy the same dimension and that's when everything will go kablooey.'

'Kablooey?'

'Sorry, scientific term. It just means every atom of every thing you have ever known will explode at the same time, noisily and probably quite painfully.'

'Oh no.'

'But the good news is I think we can stop it. I think we can reverse the WayDoor so it becomes an exit instead of an entrance. I think that will draw all the ABCs back into their own dimension, and then shut the door. And I think we can do it with this.'

He patted El Jirafa Tremendo meaningfully.

'My guitar?' I said.

'And science,' said the professor, as if that explained everything.

'That doesn't explain anything,' I said. 'How is my guitar going to save the world?'

'By opening a door in reality. We open doors in reality here all the time, using SCIENCE!' exclaimed Whizz. 'But this time it wasn't us who opened the door. It was you.'

'Me?'

'Yes, you, at precisely 11.15 this morning.'

'Me?' I said again. It was one thing being told I might be able to save the world. It was another thing to be told the whole thing might have been my fault in the first place.

'Yeah, think about it. What were you doing at 11.15 this morning?'

'Band practice.'

'Exactly!'

'Exactly?'

'Yes, exactly,' he said, pulling out a battered yellow gizmo from his pocket. 'See?' he said.

'Well, I can see a battered yellow gizmo, yes.'

'Exactly. It's my oddometer. It measures oddness.' He pointed at a glass panel in the middle of the oddometer. It had a circular dial in it with a pointer that quivered like the needle of a compass. Around the outside of the dial was tiny writing.

'So you can see that the needle is currently hovering between "hmm, that's weird" and "batpoop crazy". Which I think you'll agree is pretty darned accurate. Normally it would be down around "mildly eccentric" or "a bit rum". But at 11.15 this morning it peaked at "WOOP WOOP IT'S ALL GONE PROPER BONKERS" and gave the coordinates for the Community Centre. That's why I was there this morning, researching.'

'Stealing my guitar.'

'Borrowing it. Anyhoo, I think at that precise moment you did something in the Community Centre, something that summoned a OneWay Wild Wandering WayDoor. A wild, roaming rift between our dimension and the dimension of the ABCs. So. What were you doing when the ABCs appeared outside the Community Centre?'

'We were playing music. I was just trying out a new chord. F minus.'

'F minus? Wow. I do not know that one. OK, I think we can stop this. All we need to do is get you to play whatever you were playing at precisely 11.15 this morning. That should conjure the door, then I'll just zap it with a blast of my particular speciality, which is,' and at this point he brought up both hands with their thumbs up and shouted, 'SCIENCE! And then problemo solved-o. Door fixed. World saved.'

'OK!' I said. 'OK, that sounds like a good plan! Let's—'

There was a noise that sounded exactly like everyone in the world shouting *VAAAAAARM* at the same time, and brick and plasterwork tumbled to the floor as a big hole appeared in the wall, revealing a tall woman in Biscuit Factory overalls.

The badge on her chest read: 'Hi, I'm Tiffany. Ask me about our Nutty Flapjacks!'

'Everybody stop what they are doing,' she said. Her voice was deep and commanding, so we would probably have done what she said even if she hadn't been carrying a big, cruel-looking gun, and even if she hadn't made it go *chuk-*

chuk by pumping it after the word 'doing' and even if the gun wasn't pointing at us, but she was and she did and it was, so we did.

Chapter 18

VAAAARM

Tiffany was a bit like the Terminator, I thought. All big and cold and robotic and scary. I had just started to wonder whether that made her a Tiffanator or a Terminiffany when she started talking again.

'You need to put the guitar down,' she said, pointing her gun at Whizz.

'You need to get on the next Happybus home,' she said, pointing her gun at me.

'And you . . .' she faltered, looking at Man Man, 'you appear to be some kind of superhero and I'm not sure how to deal with that, so I'm just going to ignore you if that's OK.'

Which was exactly typical of the Biscuit Factory way of doing things. I didn't think that ignoring Man Man was going to be a good strategy for her in the long run, but I said nothing because I was a little worried that she might shoot me if I did.

'OK, so, hi Tiffany,' said the professor, with an enormously charming smile. 'We're actually quite close to working out how to sort out this whole sort of monster situation.'

'Are you the Department for Closing Holes in Reality?' said Tiffany.

'Well, OK, so, no,' said Whizz. 'But there doesn't actually seem to be a Department for

VAAAAARM.'

He didn't actually say that, but Tiffany had interrupted him by shooting a noisy, nasty, blood-red beam at the ceiling.

'Have I got your attention?' she asked, and she absolutely did have.

Bits of tiling and pipework landed on the

ground around us.

'It's time to tidy up this place,' said Man Man under his breath.

I panicked slightly because if the next sentence was a rhyme . . .

'By punching evil in the face,' continued Man Man, raising his paws in a menacing manner. He took a step towards Tiffany.

'Get back.' Tiffany aimed her gun at the rabbit. The scary thing about it was there was no emotion in her voice, it was simply an instruction. An instruction that Man Man ignored.

'So evil-doers better run . . .'

VAAAAAAARM

'. . . oh heck, where has my left ear gone?'

Top marks for rhyming in extreme circumstances, I thought, but oh my gosh Tiffany had shot Man Man's ear off with a noisy, nasty, blood-red beam.

'Now look what you did,' said Tiffany.

Man Man staggered back and then sat down with a flumph.

'Are you all right?' I asked.

'Most of me, yes,' said Man Man. 'Probably 90 per cent of me is dandy. The other 10 per cent is . . . ow . . . missing. I just need a moment to recharge my man powers.'

'How could you do that?' I said to Tiffany.

'He did it to himself,' said Tiffany. 'This is the danger of doing things. Do you understand? If you understand, do nothing.'

We did nothing.

'Excellent,' said Tiffany. 'They say it is better to regret something you *did* do, rather than something you *didn't*. They are wrong, do I make myself clear?'

'Oh man, like crystal,' said Whizz. 'Like, I totally regret inventing that gun, I have to say.'

'What?' I turned to the professor. 'You invented that thing? What were you thinking?'

'Science,' said the professor glumly, as if that explained everything.

'This is the Biscuit Factory Foby gun,' said Tiffany, stroking the gun. Finally there was some emotion in her voice. It sounded a bit like love. 'A beautiful bit of kit.'

'Foby gun?'

'It's short for Foe-Be-Gone,' said the professor. 'I just had this really cool idea for a gun that would shoot noisy, nasty, blood-red beams, while making a kind of VAAAARMing sound, and before I knew it I had a working prototype. Um. Whoops?'

He smiled an embarrassed little smile.

'It is very effective,' said Man Man, gingerly prodding the blackened stump where his left ear used to be.

'Thanks, man,' said Whizz. 'I mean, sorry, also.'

'Whizz, what is wrong with you people?' I said. 'You do your science, invent stuff just for the heck of it, and then people use your inventions to shoot the ears off rabbits, or destroy the whole of reality, you plum.'

'All right, all right,' said Whizz. 'This whole situation has me totally rethinking my whole approach to inventing things and consequences and whatnot, all right? Although, on the plus side, one good thing about inventing that gun is that I know it only has enough charge for three shots, and that was the third, so, you know. Every cloud and all that.'

'Her gun is decharged just as my man powers have recharged!' said Man Man, rising unsteadily to his feet. 'When evil's gun is out of vaaarm, it's time to do her face some harm!'

'Woah woah woah, can we talk about this instead?' I said. 'Man Man, wait a sec. Tiffany, we're just trying to save the world here, so . . .'

But Tiffany had thrown her Foby gun to the ground and adopted a kind of kung fu stance, which to my mind wasn't how you arranged yourself if you wanted a reasonable chat.

'Seriously, are you two just going to fight, is

that what's happening here?' I said. 'Because how is that going to solve anything?'

But my plea fell on deaf ears, or, in Man Man's case, ear.

They circled each other, sizing each other up.

'Man Man, it's not very heroic to hit a woman!' I mean, it wasn't particularly heroic to hit anyone, but Man Man seemed to have an old-fashioned outlook on heroism, so it was worth a try.

Tiffany never broke eye contact with the rabbit as she spoke: 'I am not a woman, I'm a duly designated security officer of the Biscuit Factory.'

'I think that means I'm off the hook, heroically speaking,' said Man Man. 'She's pretty much admitted to being a henchman. Henchwoman. Hench—'

He didn't get a chance to finish his thought because Tiffany aimed a twirling kick at his adorably fuzzy head, he ducked just in time, and battle commenced.

'Can we stop this?' I said to Whizz, who just

shrugged unhappily.

'Haddie, we need to get out of here. Now Tiffany's found us there'll be more Biscuitrons along any minute. Time is not on our side. I have a secret laboratory in town where we can experiment with your guitar, and *excuse me . . .*'

He stepped aside as Tiffany tottered past, desperately trying to tug two angry metres of rabbit off her face. They slammed into a wall, Man Man was dislodged and the fight continued.

'Where was I?' continued Whizz. 'Oh yeah, so if you could break up the fight, I'll get us out of here.'

'Break up the— *excuse me*,' I said, stepping aside as Man Man and Tiffany bundled past us again, Tiffany holding Man Man at arm's length by his one ear, Man Man kicking out with his red-booted bunny legs.

'Break up the fight?' I continued. 'And how exactly am I going to do that?'

'Use your weapon,' said Whizz and he pointed at El Jirafa.

WOAH YEAH!

And with that he scurried towards the back of the room.

I looked down at El Jirafa. In many ways a guitar is a perfect weapon. You can swing it around your head like a big, blunt battleaxe, or you can jab people with the headstock, or you can accidentally leave it lying around on the floor outside the kitchen where your mum can trip over it, spilling her hot mug of turmeric yuckymuck all over the carpet. Oh yes. You can certainly do some damage with a guitar if you use it right.

But if you really want to stop someone in their tracks using a guitar, the best way is to plug it in, turn it up and bang out a tune so awesome that people just can't help but stop and listen.

I knew just the song.

I fished in my back pocket for a plectrum, found one, grasped it, lifted my hand into the air.

I expect the plectrum glinted in the fluorescent

166

light. I don't know, I was looking down at the guitar because I couldn't play it without looking at it.

I murmured under my breath:

'A-one, a-two, a-one two three four!'

And I brought the plectrum down in a swooping movement and dragged it across El Jirafa Tremendo's six strings.

SKA-DANNNⁿNNNⁿNNG! went El Jirafa.

I did it again.

SKA-DANNⁿNNNⁿNNⁿNG!

And then I sang:

'OH HECK LONG NECK EL JIRAFA EL JIRAFA'

SKA-DANNNⁿNNNⁿNNG!

'ONE TWO CHECK CHECK EL JIRAFA EL JIRAFA'

SKA-DANNNⁿNNⁿNNⁿNG!

It was a song called, 'Oh Heck Long Neck El Jirafa'.

What's it about, Haddie? you ask.

To which I reply: it's about two minutes long.

But I didn't need to play the whole thing. By

the time I got to the fourth EL JIRAFA Tiffany and
Man Man had stopped fighting and were staring
at me. It was kind of beautiful. A hush descended
over us. My guitar, my music, had bestowed
peace upon the Earth, or at least this corner of
the room, and brought unity where there had
been discord.

WOAH YEAH!

'That was the worst thing I have ever heard,'
said Tiffany.

'I almost wish you'd shot *both* my ears off,' said
Man Man.

And they started laughing. They creased, they
held their stomachs, they laughed with tears
rolling down their cheeks.

'All right, all right,' I said.

The main thing was they had stopped fighting.
The fact they clearly knew NOTHING about good
music wasn't my problem.

'Hey, you guys,' said Professor Whizz. 'Surf's
up.'

He was holding a surfboard, the same board

that he'd flown on when he stole El Jirafa.

He flipped it out from under his arm. It twisted in the air, spun three times then came to rest a metre from the ground, where it hovered.

'Hop on,' he said with a smile.

I unplugged El Jirafa and slung her around so she clung to my back and I stepped on to the board. It dipped gently with my weight, then settled again, maintaining its distance from the ground.

'Excuse me,' said Tiffany.

Professor Whizz jumped on behind me.

'Now let's catch a wave,' he said.

'Step down from the surfboard,' said Tiffany.

'But there's no water here,' I said.

'This is no ordinary surfboard. It's a MoodBoard. It surfs on waves of emotion. Waves of disapproval, waves of hostility, waves of disappointment . . . can you feel it?'

'Please will you stop ignoring me,' said Tiffany.

Under my feet the MoodBoard wiggled.

'I repeat, step down from the surfboard.'

The MoodBoard jiggled.

'Hey Man Man, you coming?' said Whizz.

'Don't you dare,' said Tiffany, as Man Man hopped over on to the board.

The MoodBoard bucked.

'I absolutely insist that you stop doing whatever you are doing!' said Tiffany, and that apparently generated a big enough wave of frustration for the board to catch and

WA-ZAZZOOOOOOOOM!

We surfed right past her, through the hole in the wall and into the corridor.

Chapter 19

BA-DAMM

'Wa-hooooo!' I shouted, because there didn't seem to be anything else worth saying.

You know that feeling when you're flying at the speed of elation down a narrow corridor, with the wind in your hair and a guitar round your neck? This felt exactly like that.

We hung a left and headed down the corridor.

We passed doors marked 'Unstable Breaches', 'Shimmering Rifts', 'Glowing Portals' and 'Uncanny Cat Flaps'.

'What exactly do you do in here?' I asked.

'We make biscuits,' the professor said.

'You absolutely do not!'

'Well, we made one. We had to, otherwise legally we couldn't call ourselves the Biscuit Factory. And once we'd made a biscuit we were free to do what we were actually brought together to do, which is to explore the possibilities of interdimensional travel. We are experts in opening and navigating the pathways and wormholes between dimensions. Uh, which is the way out again?'

'Reception is behind us,' I said.

'Nuts,' he said. 'Hold on.'

I wasn't sure whether we were going to bank left or right, so I held on as tight as I could, which was lucky as it turned out we were going up and over in a swift loop-the-loop.

WA-ZAZZOOOOOOOOM!

'Wa-hoo!' I shouted again because this was probably the best thing that had happened to me so far today.

'Yeah, so our universe is only one of literally loads of universes in loads of dimensions making up the Big Assortment Box of Reality. We use science to open gateways between those dimensions and pop our heads in, have a rummage, see what's what. The trouble is, we've been doing it for a while and that means the walls between dimensions are a bit weaker in Normalton than in other places. Which is why you were able to open a door with the vibrations caused by your music, I think.'

'So . . . this wasn't my fault?' I said, a little relieved.

'Well, not entirely. It was a joint effort,' said Whizz, beaming. He lifted up a hand. 'High five for team . . . BRACE YOURSELVES!'

'What? Why?'

Ba-DAMM!

We burst through the door at the end of the corridor, and into Maureen's lair.

'Hold on!' shouted the professor, as the board banked and wove its way to the exit door.

I caught a blurry glimpse of Maureen as we zoomed past her. She was tapping her favourite key on the keyboard in front of her, a puzzled expression on her face. She did not react to the flying surfboard with a girl, a rabbit and a scientist on it doing a fly-by, because nobody had told her it was happening.

Ba-DAMM!

'Brace yourselves!' shouted the professor. 'Sorry, I probably should have said that before we hit the door.'

And we were out, out of the factory and soaring, higher and higher over Carpenter's Hill.

'This is AMAZING!' I said. Looking down on the trees that covered Carpenter's Hill, I could see Dead Man's Curvy, and then the outskirts of town and then we were up above the streets and houses of Normalton.

It looked so peaceful from up here. Then I realised that was most likely because everybody was sitting at home waiting for a rescue operation that was never going to happen.

I could see four or five bright red Happybuses trundling the streets, no doubt ferrying stragglers and reassuring them that everything was going to be all right.

And all over town were fuzzy orange blobs – in the middle of roads, on lawns, on top of cars, or the roofs of houses. ABCs everywhere you looked.

I felt a slight pang of guilt – hadn't the professor made it clear that this mess was at least partially my fault?

Still, I thought, I was going to be the one to sort it all out again, so maybe that made it even.

'Man Man, Man Man, flying like a man can't,' sang Man Man. He was clearly enjoying himself.

And why not? We were flying on a surfboard. I had a guitar strapped around my neck, and the wind was whipping through my hair. But there was something missing.

I missed my friends.

I missed Naomi. How cool would she have looked, standing on a flying surfboard? So cool, so unflappable. And that would have stopped the flapping in my stomach, which currently felt like it was hosting a convention for butterflies with a flapping addiction.

And I missed George. He would have absolutely hated this, I thought. He would have worried and complained about heights and speed and falling and being shot at for the whole trip, and I would have reassured him, and he would have been reassured for about thirty seconds before worrying again and that would have reassured me that everything was good, everything was normal and oh my goodness did we still have three hours to save the world or was it more like two and a half now?

'Where are we heading? Are we nearly there?' I asked Whizz.

'I just live on the south side, we're about a minute away, as the surfer flies.'

Womwomwom.

I recognised that sound.

All the little hairs on my arms stood on end as a large set of double doors appeared out of nowhere about fifty metres in front of the

MoodBoard, all lime-green-crackly, squeezing out another orange furry monster.

'Evasive manoeuvres!' shouted the Professor, which is a great thing to shout when you need to take evasive manoeuvres, and I totally understand why he shouted it, but I guess the lesson we were just about to learn was this:

If you have time to either a) *take* evasive manoeuvres or b) *shout*, 'Evasive manoeuvres' then you should a) take evasive manoeuvres every time, because if you don't then you find yourself involved in what scientists call 'an airborne ABC/person interaction', i.e. you get hit in the MoodBoard by a Bumblefluff and you go down hard.

Which is what happened to us right after the Professor shouted, 'Evasive manoeuvres' like a plum.

Chapter 20

WA-ZAZZOOOOOOM

We collided with the big, stupid, orange thing with a *WA-PLUMPH* and we were all knocked off the MoodBoard.

Occasionally you will read a book in which a character has a slight sinking feeling. Right now I was wishing that I *did* have a slight sinking feeling, rather than the extreme plummeting feeling that I was having, a feeling that was almost certainly being caused by the plummeting I was doing.

At least I wasn't alone. Man Man, Whizz and the Bumblefluff were plummeting with me, as was the MoodBoard.

It looked hopeless, unless you were hoping to hit the ground, which I was not.

If anything, I was more hoping not to hit the ground.

The wind whippled and flapped at my hair and my clothes and I thought, well this is it, should I close my eyes or keep them open and what's it going to feel like when I hit the ground and, oh, look at the way the sunlight catches the edges of the MoodBoard as it falls next to me and isn't it pretty and I think this is probably going to hurt a lot and . . .

I can't really explain what happened next, but something inside me said *No, I don't want to fall.* And then it said *Yes, I can do something about this* and before I knew what was happening I had reached out and grabbed the edge of the falling MoodBoard. I grabbed it, I held tight and I created a wave.

A wave of hope, hope that I would be able to save myself and Man Man and Whizz and

even the big stupid orange thing. I didn't mean
to. I just really, really hoped we wouldn't all go
SPLATOOM on the ground, which is a perfectly
reasonable hope, isn't it?

The MoodBoard wiggled in my hand. It jiggled.
It bucked. And then

WA-ZAZZOOOOOOOOM!

It powered up, caught the wave of hope and
got to work, swooping, soaring, diving and

WA-ZAZZOOOOOOOOM-ing.

As I clung on for dear life, the MoodBoard
scooped Man Man out of the air, did a one-
eighty, swept Whizz up, performed a perfect
barrel roll which, if I was being critical, was a
bit cocky, like it was scoring points for artistic
merit as well as technical performance, and then
positioned itself perfectly to pluck the falling
orange Bumblefluff out of the sky, at which point
it slowed enough for us all to find our feet and
catch our breath, and Whizz hauled me up on to
the deck of the board, between Man Man and the
ridiculous orange thing, which was just sitting

smiling like an idiot.

'Woah,' said Whizz. 'That was intense. Let's do it again!'

I think he was joking.

'You are the greatest team-up partner a man could have,' said Man Man.

'How did you do that, Haddie?' said Whizz.

'I think it was the board that did it, not me,' I said.

'That's not really how the board works. It must've caught one heck of a powerful mood wave, you can still feel it humming with whatever you threw at it,' said Whizz.

I shrugged.

'I think it was just hope,' I said. 'Hope's a mood, isn't it?'

'Mm,' said Whizz. 'But you didn't just hope, did you? You grabbed the board. You reached out and you grabbed it. It was hope and action, that's what saved us. Plus science, of course.'

'Mm,' said Man Man. 'But it wasn't just hope and action and science, was it? It was style as well. Creativity. Hot pants! You bust some major moves with this thing.'

'MM,' said the Bumblefluff. 'I AM BIG AND ORANGE.'

'Thanks for that,' I said. I'll admit, I was blushing slightly. 'But how long have we got till kablooey time? Should we stay here making lists or should we go and save the world?'

The answer was obvious, of course. I really hate making lists.

Chapter 21

BOMBOMCLATTERTHUMP

'Alpaca Waka Waka,' I said.

'Really?' said Whizz. 'And what does that mean, exactly?'

'It means,' I said, slowly and patiently, 'Alpaca Waka Waka.'

'OK,' said Whizz. 'And that's what you were singing when the One Way Wild Wandering WayDoor appeared.'

'Yes,' I said.

'Extraordinary,' said Whizz. 'And you were playing El Jirafa.'

'I was.'

'What chords?'

'Just F minus.'

'F minus is not a chord.'

'Yes, it is.'

'It's not in any of the chord books I've read.'

'Oh really. Well, none of this,' I gestured at the MoodBoard and Man Man and the Bumblefluff who were standing in the corner of Professor Whizz's Whizzcave, 'is in any of the science books I've read, so . . .'

'Point taken,' said Whizz.

Whizz's Whizzcave was actually just the garage of Whizz's house. He kept a vintage Raleigh Chopper bike, some rusty garden furniture and a pile of big, black guitar amplifiers in there. He also currently had a furry superhero and a big orange goober which had resisted our every attempt to get it off the MoodBoard in there, too. It was basically a standard garage, full of weird, out-of-place things that you hope might come in useful one day.

And I include myself in that description.

Frankly I'm surprised you weren't in there, too.

We had plugged El Jirafa into the amplifier, Whizz had strapped on a bass guitar and he'd raided his kitchen for a set of Tupperware that more or less resembled George's drum kit.

'See, I was telling you about how we do things in the Factory,' said Whizz. 'We do science and open portals between dimensions. What you've achieved is a little different. You appear to have generated your own door using . . . well, creativity.'

'Maybe the door was opened by God, providing an exit for anyone unfortunate enough to hear her music,' piped up Man Man. 'What?'

'Not helpful, man,' said Whizz.

Man Man shrugged.

'Haddie, I like you a whole lot, but your music is an utter aural catastrophe,' he said.

'You sound like my mum,' I said.

Oh gosh, Mum! In all this world-saving, I'd forgotten to check up on her. She was probably all right, it's not like she would have gone outside or anything, but still. I made a mental note to check on her ASAP.

'I mean, it's only half as bad as it could be, I suppose, but then I only have one ear,' muttered Man Man to himself.

'Anyhoo, my theory is, if we replicate the exact noise you made in the Community Centre this morning, you should summon the One Way Wild Wandering WayDoor. And if we can do THAT then I'll be able to adjust the polarity of the door with a quick squirt of science and bingo bongo, the way in to our world becomes the way out and the ABCs should be sucked back into their own dimension.'

'A quick squirt of science?'

'Oh yes, the science is the easy bit. We've been using science to control portals for yonks. The hard bit is predicting where the WayDoor will pop up, and we need to know where it will be so we can be there, too. Up to now it was impossible to predict, but with you playing that should be easy – it'll pop up wherever you make that sound. So, Maestro,' said Whizz. 'What do you want us to play? What were you playing when it all kicked off?'

I showed Whizz the note he was to play on the bass, and I showed Man Man which specific items of Tupperware he was supposed to bang.

Then I fished in my back pocket and found a plectrum. I nervously placed my fingers on the fret, lifted the plectrum and closed my eyes.

'Are you ready?' said the professor.

'I . . . I think so.'

'Then let's save the world, shall we?'

I lifted my right hand, the one holding the plectrum. I expect it glinted in the fluorescent light. I don't know, I still had my eyes closed.

'Ready? A-one, a-two, a-one two three four!'

And I brought the plectrum down in a swooping movement and dragged it across El Jirafa's six strings.

SKA-DANNNNNNNNNNG! went El Jirafa.
'ALPACA WAKA WAKA,' went me.
BOMBOMBOM went Whizz's bass.

CLATTERTHUMPA! went Man Man on the drums.

Yeah, that was the sound. It surrounded me and enveloped me. It entered me and gave all my internal organs a rattle. Classic F minus. I opened my eyes, exhaled and smiled at the professor.

Saving the world with my song. No feeling like it.

'It is done,' I said. 'What should I be looking out for? How do we know if it worked?'

'It didn't work,' said the professor.

Chapter 22

SIGH

'According to my calculations, if you were genuinely the cause of the One Way Wild Wandering WayDoor, it should have appeared by now,' said Whizz. 'And it didn't.'

'Oh, OK,' I said, a little deflated. 'Should we try again? Maybe louder.'

'No!' said Man Man. 'I've never wanted to punch anything so badly as I've wanted to punch that song, but it doesn't have a face. I am powerless against it. Your music is my kryptonite.'

'Haha, so I wouldn't put it like that,' said Whizz, 'but honestly, Haddie, we tried and it didn't work.

Something in my calculations is off.'

'So what do we do now?'

'First of all, we look on the bright side. Guess what? This means you didn't open the WayDoor. None of this is your fault. High five!'

He raised his palm, a bit optimistically.

'But it also means I can't save the world.'

'Yeah, well, look . . .' He lowered his un-fived palm. 'I need to get back to the Biscuit Factory to . . . I don't know, maybe I can work out exactly what caused the door, and . . . I mean, I'm not sure what I can do but I'm sure I'll think of something.'

'And what about me?'

'Right. You can . . . I mean probably the best thing you can do is to do something you enjoy doing for the next, ah . . .' He looked at his watch. 'Ninety minutes or so. And all the minutes you'll have after that, of course, but I do recommend you really, really try to enjoy the next hour and a half. You and El Jirafa.'

There was nothing I could do. I was useless.

'When all this is over we'll look back and laugh!' said Whizz. He had hopped on his MoodBoard and was floating out through the front of his garage. The big orange Bumblefluff sat on the back smiling inanely.

I sighed. The MoodBoard wiggled, jiggled, bucked and then . . .

WA-ZAZOOOOOM.

Off it shot, no doubt surfing the wave of my own disappointment. At least that was useful, I thought.

I sighed again. So this is how the world ends, I thought. With a sigh and a shrug. And a massive kablooey of course.

I shrugged.

'What about you?' I said to Man Man. 'What are you doing now? Fancy hanging around with me?'

'Will you be pestering the giraffe?' he said, gesturing at El Jirafa. 'Making it make those noises?'

'I suppose, yes. What else is there to do?'

'OK, well, this has been a titanic team-up, but I think it's time we went solo for a bit,' he said. 'Hey, I might go see what Tiffany's up to. Maybe we can have a climactic battle or something. You know, throwing each other around while the world ends around us. You're welcome to join us.'

'No, I think I'll just go and get the bus home,' I said. 'But thank you for the offer.'

'OK. Until next we meet! When foes endanger the many, it's time to punch a Tiffany!' and he shot off, out of the garage, in the general direction of Dead Man's Curvy and the Biscuit Factory.

I envied him a little. At least he was going to do what he loved doing, i.e. knocking people about with his fists. I was just going to go home and sit tight and hope that someone, anyone, would save this stupid world, because there was absolutely nothing I could do.

I slung El Jirafa around on her strap so she clung to my back and went to find a Happybus that would take me home.

Chapter 23

DEE DI DI DEE DI DI DEE DI DI DEEE

I waited at the bus stop for ten minutes and watched as three bright red Happybuses with 'Everything is All Right' plastered across their sides trundled past, none of them so much as slowing down.

'They won't stop, you know.'

There was a Biscuitron standing behind me, wearing beige overalls, and a badge that read: 'Hi, I'm Toby. Ask me about our Coconutties!'

'What makes you say that?'

'They're driverless. And they're controlled by a central computer in the Biscuit Factory. A central computer that's currently being sat on by a big orange ABC. They'll just trundle around aimlessly until they run out of fuel.'

'Oh,' I said. 'I know how they feel.'

VAAAAARM.

The bus stop disappeared in a noisy, nasty, blood-red beam.

Jeepers! He had a Foby gun. I quickly checked my arms, legs, head, etc., but he didn't seem to have been shooting at me.

VAAAAARM he

went again. This time I saw the noisy, nasty, blood-red beam shoot out and hit a tree, which more or less turned into a pile of pencil sharpenings.

'What the heckin heck are you doing?' I shouted at Toby.

'Having fun. The whole place is going kablooey soon anyhow, so where's the harm? I've got one shot left. What shall I aim it at?'

I had a couple of ideas but what was the point?

Womwomwom.

I recognised that sound.

All the little hairs on my arms stood on end as a large set of double doors appeared out of nowhere.

I barely noticed it.

It was becoming normal.

I just walked away from Toby and the remains of the bus stop, as much to avoid having to look at another stupid, big, orange Bumblefluff as for any other reason.

This was Normalton's new normal. Stupid buses, empty streets, Biscuitrons amusing themselves and huge orange dingdongs everywhere you looked. I could barely be bothered to get vexed about it.

I trudged home, only ever quickening my pace when I heard a *wom*-ing.

I was sick of the weirdness of the normality of the outside world.

I needed the comfort of the weirdness of the normality of Mum and home.

'Mum, I'm home,' I said as I walked in the front door. I leaned El Jirafa against the wall.

'Hi, love,' said Mum. Her voice was a bit distant and a bit muffled.

'Mum, where are you?'

'I'm just in the cupboard, lovey.'

'What are you looking for?'

'What do you mean, lovey?'

I walked into the living room. Normally, there would be a candle flickering merrily on the coffee table smelling of serenity or enlightenment or cake. Normally, there would be a bowl of snacks that looked like wood chippings or grass cuttings or toenails. Normally, my mum would be stretching out on the sofa or planking on the rug or reading a book called *You Are The Best You* or *The Little Book of Calm Down Pet* or *I Can Make You Buy This Book!*

Instead there were three big, orange, fluffy monsters, one on the sofa, one on the coffee table and one on the one on the sofa. There was no room for anything else.

'Mum?' I said. 'Mum, where are you?'

'I'm still in the cupboard, Haddie.'

We had an understairs cupboard where we kept the Hoover and bits of the old Hoover and a stockpile of old shoes. I ran to it. It was closed. I tried to open it but it wouldn't.

'Mum, are you in here?'

'Yes, I am.'

'Well, are you going to come out?'

'No, I am not.'

I sat down on the carpet.

'Mum, please, you've got to come out.'

'No, I don't think I do. I wasn't enjoying being in the living room. There's . . . there must be a draught or something.'

'Mum, there's three huge orange monsters in there but they're harmless, honestly.'

'Well, I doubt that. I just feel happier in here for now, thank you.'

'Oh, Mum. Can I get you anything? A mug of mucky turmeric or anything?'

'No, I don't think so, thank you. Don't worry about me, lovey. I'm perfectly happy in here.'

And she probably was, or at least she thought

she was, and what's the difference, really?

But I was not perfectly happy. I was perfectly NOT happy. Those plums at the Biscuit Factory had invaded my home. My weird had been changed into their weird. There was no escape from it. Nothing I could do about it. I should just sit there and do what I was told, i.e. do nothing.

They'd made my mum feel weird and unsafe in her own living room. Those utter, utter, utter . . .

I sat for a minute. But something welled up inside me, and around me.

A feeling.

I wiggled. I jiggled. I bucked. And then. And then.

I got up. There was a wave under me that I couldn't ignore.

A wave of disobedience.

You don't start a band because you want to be told what to do.

You don't play music every Saturday because that's what people WANT you to do.

You do it because you want to *do* something.

You do it because you want to *make* something. Something that's yours.

That's why I played guitar.

That's why me and Naomi and George . . .

Dee di di dee di di dee di di deeeeeeeee.

I recognised the tune that had started playing in my head.

Dee di di dee di di dee di di deee.

My brain had started to play Big Thought Tetris.

All the little multicoloured, misshapen thoughts of the day started to tumble into my brain pit, arranging themselves and dropping into place.

Dee di di dee di di dee di di deee.

George was told what to do every day at home. Smile, George. Make yourself useful, George.

George was told what to do every day at school. Sit down, George. Stand up, George.

George was told what to do . . .

Dee di di dee di di dee di di deee.

The last thought locked into place. Level up.

Oh heckins.

Oh hecky heckington.

This wasn't my fault.

This was *our* fault.

Because George *hadn't* done what he was told.

Because Naomi *hadn't* done what she was told.

So the sound we played wasn't the sound I wanted us to play.

It was the sound *we'd* wanted to play.

Whizz and Man Man had played exactly what I'd told them to play in the garage. They'd played it right.

And that was wrong.

It was wrong. And I'd been wrong. I'd told George what to do. And Naomi. Like, all the time.

I was in a band because I didn't like being told what to do. So why was George in the band? Why was Naomi? Just to be bossed around by me?

Oh no. Not only was the world about to end, I was going to have to apologise to my friends. I didn't know which was worse.

All right, I did know, of course I did, but it's not nice knowing you owe someone an apology.

I ran to the front door and picked up El Jirafa and slung her by the strap on to my back.

And then I ran back to the cupboard.

'Mum, I'm just popping out to save the world, which is sort of ending and it might be my fault, a bit. I should be back in an hour or so,' I said.

'OK, lovey,' said Mum.

'And I'm going to have to apologise to my friends as well.'

'Really?' said Mum. 'Well, that's a very brave thing to admit and to do. I'm proud of you, Haddie.'

Mums, honestly. There's nothing weirder or more wonderful.

Chapter 24

URGH OOF NNNNNG

I rang George's doorbell and waited.

'Just coming!' said the voice of Mrs George from inside the house. 'Just coming. One moment. Hang on,' she said.

I waited.

'Just coming,' she said.

I waited some more.

Womwomwom.

I recognised that sound.

All the little hairs on my arms stood on end. Somewhere nearby another ABC was entering our dimension.

I rang the doorbell again.

'Just coming!' said Mrs George, and the door opened.

The doorway was filled with a huge amount of orange fur. There were two ABCs crowding the frame, and Mrs George had somehow managed to squeeze herself between them.

'Hello, Haddie,' said Mrs George. 'How is everything? Everything is absolutely all right here, thank you for asking. No problems in this particular household.'

'Of course,' I said. 'Can I come in?'

'Um . . .' said Mrs George. 'That might be a bit difficult.'

'Why?'

'Oh . . . well I've just taken Vinny for a spin, so . . . er, we don't want you tramping dirt through the house, do we?'

'You've just taken Vinny for a . . . oh, you mean you've vacuumed?' I said. 'I think you might have missed a bit. I think I can see a bit of orange fluff on the carpet.'

'Oh, I doubt that,' said Mrs George through

gritted teeth. 'No orange fluff in here. The Vinnie Vacuum is very efficient. I'll get George for you. That would be a perfectly normal thing for me to do right now. I won't be a second. Urgh. Oof. Nnnnng.'

She grunted, groaned and strained to squeeze herself back through the mounds of orange fur and into the house.

I waited patiently.

'Urgh. Oof. Nnnnng.'

George's face appeared through the fur.

'Hey, George,' I said brightly. 'How are things in there?'

'All right,' he said.

'Not full of big orange monsters or anything?'

He sighed.

'What do you want, Haddie?'

'I just came to tell you that this is all your fault, George.'

'What? Really? Oh no.' George's face reddened, clashing horribly with the orange fur that surrounded him. That's my George, I thought.

He never could accessorise.

'It was my fault, too, George. And Naomi's. But we can stop this. We have to get together and play "Alpaca Waka Waka" again. You have to get your Tupperware and come with me right now.'

'No,' said George.

'Excellent. Out you come then,' I said, and then I realised he hadn't said 'yes', which was confusing because George always said 'yes' to me. It was one of the reasons I liked him so much.

'I think you misspelled "yes" there,' I said.

'No,' said George. 'I've had a horrible day. People have pointed at me. They told me off for things I didn't do. And it was horrible. I am tired and a bit freaked out, so I'm staying in. Maybe for ever.'

'Well, that might not be as long as you think,' I said. 'You have to come because I need you to come. I'm in a bit of a hurry, so if you could come out now, that would be great.'

'Haddie, you're not listening to me. You never

listen to me!'

'Sorry, what was that?' I said, because I can find time to be funny even when there's less than five chapters to save the world.

'You're not funny,' said George, against all the evidence. 'I really like being your friend, and we do all kinds of cool stuff but sometimes I don't want to do what you want to do, and I try to tell you that, and then we wind up doing it anyway.'

I took a deep breath.

'George, I'm sorry,' I said.

'What?'

'I'm sorry. I was wrong. I've been wrong a lot and I'm sorry and I want to make things better, and I will, and I will be a better friend and I promise I won't make you do anything you don't want to do ever again, but honestly, George, if we don't play "Alpaca Waka Waka" in the next forty-five minutes the world will end in a massive explosion destroying at least two universes in one big kablooey.'

'What?' said George. 'Really?'

I nodded.

'You're really, genuinely sorry?'

'Er. Yes.' I hadn't expected that to be the bit he questioned. Was it really easier to believe the world was going to go kablooey than to believe I was apologising?

'Urgh, oof, nnnng.' George squeezed his way out of the morass of orange fur on to the path and gave me a big hug.

'Urgh. Stop that!' I said.

'You can't make me,' he said.

So I let him hug me for a bit longer. It was nice. Then we went to find Naomi.

Chapter 25

KRAKA-DOOOOOM

'If I was motto-cool and enigmatic and really very cool, where would I be?' I said.

We had quickly realised we didn't have any idea where Naomi lived.

We were moving and we were moving fast but we weren't going in any particular direction because that's just how this day was going, generally.

'I like to imagine she hangs out on a yacht with some rappers,' said George. 'Or . . . have you checked to see if she's trending on social media somewhere?'

'OK, think. What do we know about Naomi?' I said. 'What do we REALLY know about her?'

'She's got great hair.'

'Yes. And her clothes are astonishingly cool.'

'Yes, but she never looks like she's put any effort in. And when she's got her bass guitar round her neck it doesn't even matter what she's playing, you just want to look at her hair and her clothes.'

'She is so cool!' I said, full of admiration. 'But she's never told us anything about who she really is. Or where she goes when we're not practising.'

'Have you tried the allotment?' said Man Man, which was a surprise, considering the last I'd seen him he was spoiling for a fight with Tiffany. 'Incidentally, you haven't seen Tiffany anywhere, have you?'

He was trotting alongside us. How long he'd been there was anybody's guess.

'Allotment?' I said. 'That is literally the last place you'd find a cool person like Naomi.'

'Sure, if she *was* a person,' sniffed Man Man. 'Have you seen anyone who looks like they need punching? I haven't punched anyone in ages. I'm not feeling very heroic.'

'What do you mean, *if* she was a person? Of course she's a person.'

'Er, Haddie,' said George. 'Look!'

By chance we had reached Normalton's allotments. They ran alongside the railway, all chain-link fencing, ramshackle huts, weird home-made scarecrows and rows and rows of root vegetables.

And there in the middle of a soily vegetable patch sat Naomi, hair perfect, and a middle-aged man wearing a smart suit and a tie with little fat penguins embroidered into it, munching away on a pile of carrots.

'Naomi!' I shouted.

Naomi and the man looked up, startled, and dip me in ketchup and call me a nugget ifthey didn't both start digging a hole in the soil at their feet.

'Stop, don't run away,' I cried. 'Naomi, we need you.'

'Oh lord, that's how it starts,' said the middle-aged man. 'We need you, they say. Can you sort this out, they say. What shall we do now, they say. Keep digging, Naomi, no good can come of this!'

The man had half a badge pinned to the pocket of his suit jacket, on which was written: 'Hi, I'm the Chief. Ask me about', but what exactly you were supposed to ask him about was a mystery because that bit of the badge had been snapped off.

'You're the Chief?' I said. 'You're in charge of the Biscuit Factory?'

'Oh, don't you start,' said the Chief. 'I don't want to be in charge of the Biscuit Factory. I'm digging my way out of here. Who's with me?'

'Chief, we've got some bad news,' said Man Man. 'It turns out this dimension is likely to go kablooey in the next thirty minutes. There's some situations you can't dig your way out of.'

'I can try,' said the Chief and he started digging

again, scooping out clods of earth with his hands. 'This is not my problem. I can't sort it out. We're in Crazytown. I don't even know why any of us are here. This is the worst job I've ever had.'

'Stop digging,' I said. 'Please. I'm not going to ask you to solve anything. This is our mess,' I said to Naomi. 'Yours and mine and George's. But we can sort it out, I know we can.'

Naomi sniffed, and then flicked her super-cool fringe.

'Sounds pretty motto,' she said.

'Oh, it is,' I said, smiling. 'It's *motto* motto. Will you help?'

Naomi sighed. She reached up to the back of her head and tugged at something. And then the top of her head fell off which, I'll be honest, was overly motto even for the way today had been going.

It took a second before I realised she'd just pulled a wig off. Her perfect, oh-so-cool hair – it wasn't real! And that's when I noticed her ears. They'd been hidden under the wig and they were . . . long. Really long. And furry. And brown.

And that's when I noticed her face. Like, really noticed. And I realised that I'd just seen Naomi as a perfect picture of coolness, which meant I'd never really looked at her before.

And now I was looking properly, it was pretty clear that Naomi's face was beautiful.

And brown.

And furry.

And her eyes were black and shiny. Her pink nose twitched.

Oh. She was a rabbit.

And she looked

So

Heckin'

COOL.

'You're a rabbit,' I said, and she just looked at me, like, 'duh'.

'How did I not know you were a rabbit? How did I not realise she was a rabbit? Is she . . . like, do you two know each other?' I asked Man Man.

'Listen,' he said. 'When I was dragged to this dimension by the Biscuit Factory, I wasn't alone. There were around twenty of us. They tried keeping us locked up in there while they worked out how to send us back, but we rabbits are very good at three things. Well,' he coughed, 'actually *four* things, but one of them's not relevant right now. We are good at digging our way out of things, we are good at running away. And we are very good at camouflaging ourselves. Because life as a rabbit is nasty and brutish and short unless you can master those three skills, I don't care what dimension you're from.'

'But I mean, she's so obviously a rabbit. A big rabbit, to be sure, but seriously, how did I not realise she was a big rabbit in a wig?'

'A big rabbit in a wig?' said Naomi. 'Is that what I am now?'

'No, no, Naomi, no,' I said. 'You're our bass player. And my friend. And also, sidebar: you're still cooler than a fridge wearing sunglasses. I just feel like . . . shouldn't I have noticed you were a rabbit?'

'Well, you never noticed me being an unhappy drummer,' said George. 'Maybe you're just not that observant.'

'Yeah but I noticed Man Man was a rabbit and . . .'

'Ah but I wasn't wearing my Man-glasses when you first saw me,' said Man Man. 'If I had been you'd have been as oblivious as everyone else in this dimension. All of you here would much rather not notice things if it makes your life easier. Noticing things takes effort, and raises questions that it might be simpler to leave unasked. If you had noticed Naomi was a rabbit then there'd be all kinds of other questions that would have to be answered. Like: how, or why? Same if you'd noticed George was unhappy. It's just simpler not to notice. That's why everybody in this town is working really hard to ignore the ABCs.'

'I'm sorry for never taking the time to get to know who you really are, Naomi.'

'Oh, you know who I am,' said Naomi, as she put her wig back on. 'I'm your friend. And your bass player. I'll help. Because I like it here, a lot, and I don't want the Factory to send me back. That's why I ran away from the Community Centre when Blankley turned up. I'm sorry for abandoning you. Whatever needs doing, I'll do it.'

'Don't do it!' shouted the Chief.

'What's your story?' I said. 'If you're the Chief, why aren't you helping sort things out?'

'When I escaped I just wanted to fit in!' wailed the Chief. 'So I stole an interesting tie and some Biscuit Factory overalls and did my best to not be noticed. But they kept chuckling at my funny tie and giving me new, bigger job titles, but I never knew what I was supposed to be doing, so I just did nothing, and because I didn't do anything bad they would promote me again. And now I'm Chief! I never wanted to be Chief. And then this whole ABC thing happened and everyone was asking me what we should do and I didn't know what anyone should do, so I locked the door of my office and just dug my way out. And now here I am, sitting in the soil, eating a carrot. I like it here.'

'Wow,' said Man Man, his voice full of admiration. 'I thought I was doing a good job of being a man, going round punching things and occasionally farting, but you have got the whole being a man thing *nailed*. High five!'

He lifted a paw, and maybe the Chief fived him and maybe he didn't, but to be honest although this was all very interesting, it wasn't getting the world saved.

KRAKA-DOOOOOOOOM.

For a split second the allotment was lit by a fiery orange light, and tangerine crackles arced and spat across the sky.

'I'm no scientist but this doesn't look good,' I said. 'We need to get to the Community Centre and play a song, and we need to do it now,' I said. And then, remembering my little chat with George earlier, I added, 'If everyone else is up for

217

playing a song and saving the world, that is. I mean, I don't want to force anyone.'

'I'm in,' said George. 'This is my world, and I would like it to not go kablooey.'

'You're the best, George,' I said.

'It's my world, too, now,' said Naomi. 'So, yeah, you know?'

'That's my girl,' I said. So cool!

'I'll come and help,' said the Chief. 'But you'll have to tell me exactly what to do. I refuse to make any decisions.'

'I like your attitude,' I said to him. 'Of course you can come. Man Man?'

'When the world is in danger, call a face re-arranger,' he said. 'I mean, I'm hoping to be able to punch someone, and you seem to attract the attention of extremely punchable people, so yes, I'm in.'

KRAKA-DOOOOOOOOM.

We were once again lit by a fierce orange flash, as lightning split the sky. This time, though, the glow didn't fade, and the lighting's jagged lines remained, making it look like the sky was cracked.

'This is looking bad! How long have we got?' I cried.

'Not quite long enough would be my guess,' said Man Man. 'It's a titanic battle against the odds! Hot tub! This is superhero heaven!'

'The sky is breaking! It's unthinkable that we could do anything that would make a difference,' said the Chief.

Unthinkable?

No such thing, I thought.

'Let's get to the Community Centre right now!'

'You there, stop what you're doing right now!'

The voice was cruel and nasal, like . . . well, like Blankley. It was Blankley. And he'd brought reinforcements, including . . .

'Tiffany!' cried Man Man, gleefully. 'Am I glad to see you!'

Chapter 26

HHHHHHHHHHS

The allotment was surrounded by Biscuitrons, each one holding a Foby gun.

KRAKA-DOOOOOOOM! went the heavens. The ground rumbled as another crack opened in the sky.

This was terrible.

'This is brilliant!' said Man Man. 'Hot takes! A proper climactic battle. Finally we can settle this whole thing, man to Man Man.'

'Man Man, this isn't helpful.'

'Of course it is! I'll punch Tiffany, and then Blankley, and then . . .'

'And then what? What happens when you've punched everybody?'

'Then we will be victorious!' he shouted. 'Tiffany, let's get ready to . . .'

Chuk-CHUK!

All the Biscuitrons pumped their Foby guns at exactly the same time. It was like the best and the worst drum-fill I had ever heard in my life. The sound echoed menacingly around the allotment.

'Chief,' I said. 'You can stop this. Take charge! Chief?'

I looked around.

'He's in a hole, Haddie,' said George. 'It's quite a big hole. Like, with room for all of us?'

'We're not getting in the hole, George,' I said, then, remembering certain lessons I'd learned today: 'Unless you'd like to wait in a hole until the world ends?'

'Um . . .' George was weighing up his options. 'No, no. Are they going to start shooting at us, do you think?'

'Don't worry,' I said. 'I've been shot at a few times today. You get used to it.'

YOU HAVE 1 NEW NOTIFICATION: A MESSAGE ABOUT GETTING USED TO BEING SHOT AT

You don't.

'All is lost!' wailed the Chief from inside his hole. Clods of earth flew left and right. He was clearly still digging.

Man Man was squaring up to Tiffany.

'Drop your weapon,' said Man Man. 'Let's settle this like men.'

'I'm not a man,' said Tiffany. 'I'm a duly designated security officer of the Biscuit Factory and I have my orders. Stop doing things or we'll shoot you. All of you.'

KRAKA-DOOOOOM!

More cracks appeared in the sky.

'What? You'd really shoot us? How is that going

222

to help anyone?'

'It's not about helping. It's about doing what you're told!' said Blankley. 'And what you're being told to do is nothing. What could be easier to do than that?'

'Chief,' I shouted. 'Please. They're trying to stop us doing things. You're their boss. Tell them to stop stopping us.'

'They're just following Biscuit Factory rules. There's nothing I can do about that.'

'You could change the rules!'

'I can't, the rules forbid it.'

'You're a leader!'

'I'm not, I'm a rabbit! I admit it, OK? I'm a rabbit! Which means I don't have to do what anyone tells me any more.'

Good for you, I thought. Wouldn't it be better if there were more rabbits around refusing to follow stupid orders? I scanned the ranks of Biscuitrons. Just people, like you, like me, just people, holding massively powerful guns, doing what they were told. People, with faces like . . .

well . . . some of them were a little fuzzy. Actually, now I looked at them properly, some of their faces were really fuzzy.

KRAKA-DOOOOM!

. . . a bolt of orange lightning struck a ramshackle shed to our left. It exploded into matchsticks . . .

And also **WOAH YEAH!**

. . . a bolt of hot inspiration struck me. An idea so ridiculous it absolutely HAD to be right.

I strode up to where Man Man was squaring up to the Biscuitrons.

'Oho, are you ready for another team-up?' he said. 'Itching to get fisty-fighty with these foes?'

'No,' I said and I plucked his Man-glasses off his face.

'NO!' he shouted. 'No, don't do that!'

Tiffany looked on, her face finally betraying some emotion.

'You're . . . you're a rabbit?'

'Yes, yes, he's a rabbit. He was just pretending to be a man,' I said. 'Big reveal. Surprise surprise. Now, I have a very important question for all of you. Hands up if you're a rabbit.'

I looked around the allotment. I looked pointedly at Naomi.

'Naomi, this is important,' I said.

Naomi rolled her eyes, struck a pose and tentatively raised her hand.

'Two rabbits,' I said. 'Chief?'

A small hand appeared from the hole the Chief had been digging and waved.

'I never wanted any of this,' he wailed.

'Three rabbits.'

I looked over at the Biscuitrons.

'Now come on, be honest,' I said. 'Hands up if you're a rabbit.'

A man wearing a distinctive woolly hat and the badge: 'Hi, I'm Barry. Ask me about our Custard Flumps!' raised his hand.

'I admit, I stole the uniform and the hat and made my own badge! I just thought it would be a good place to hide, keep my head down, and then suddenly they give me a gun and tell me to start shooting people but they never really told me why,' he said apologetically.

And now I looked at him properly his face beneath the bobble hat was white with a black patch over one pink eye. Textbook rabbit.

A woman in a massive scarf and the badge: 'Hi, I'm Bethany, ask me about our Cheeky Choccy Nib Nobs!' raised her hand.

'Me too! And I didn't dare ask in case they guessed I didn't really know what was going on,' she said.

How had nobody noticed the four prominent chisel-like incisors at the front of her mouth? Or her whiskers? Was her scarf really so distracting? What was wrong with this dimension?

A Biscuitron with the badge: 'Hi, I'm Mrs Fluffywhiskers. Ask me about our Carrot Cakes!' raised their hand.

'I thought my name would be a dead giveaway but because they gave me a uniform and a gun, nobody seemed to question it,' he said. 'Mrs Fluffywhiskers! I'm not even married."

Tiffany looked aghast. 'You're all rabbits?'

she said.

'I'm not,' a man with the badge: 'Hi, I'm Cyril, ask me about our Cranberry Crunches!' said. 'At least, as far as I know. I'm starting to wonder, because if I'm honest,' and here he dropped his voice to a conspiratorial whisper, 'I know literally doodly-squat about our Cranberry Crunches, so please don't ask.'

Tiffany turned on Cyril. 'We don't make any heckin' Cranberry Crunches, we're a Super-Secret Science Lab in disguise!'

Cyril mulled this over for a moment.

'Are we? Wow. Good disguise,' he said. 'I had no idea.'

KRAKA-DOOOOOOM!

'Half of you are rabbits!' I said. 'Half of you are humans! And one of you is not super-certain which he is!'

'That's me!' said Cyril.

I thought about what to say next.

'This information! Is!' I shouted. 'New! And! Very! Interesting!'

The Biscuitrons nodded expectantly. They had been waiting for so long for someone to actually take charge, they didn't seem too bothered that I was an eleven-year-old girl.

'And I don't know what to do with it!' I shouted.

There was a pause, the expressions on the faces of my audience faltered a little.

'But don't you think it should change *something*?' I said. 'You're all running around, following the rules, doing the right thing and not knowing why, and where is it getting us?'

'We should have a team-up!' shouted Man Man. 'Let's all get together, like the Avengers, or the Justice League.'

'Yes, yes, that seems like a great idea!' I said.

'And let's fight something!' he said. 'Together! Who's with me?'

The crowd erupted with a 'YEAH'.

And after the eruption there was a 'no', in a voice that sounded nasal and tired, like a tapir up way past its bedtime. It was, of course, Blankley. He said 'no' some more.

'No no no no no no,' he said. 'No. You,' he pointed at the rabbits with his finger and his face, 'are not rabbits, because you can't be. That would be ridiculous. The sky is not breaking, because it can't be. That would be insane. You are not having a team-up, because you can't be. That would be absurd. You are not doing anything about this, because you can't be, because it's not allowed and because there's no "this" to do anything about. So I can't be here, because that would be ludicrous. So you can all do what you want, as long as it's nothing, and it has nothing to do with me. I'm off.'

And he was. He walked slowly and stiffly out of the allotment. We watched him go, in silence, apart from the sound of the sky breaking. And then Tiffany broke the sort-of silence.

'We should find out whose fault all this is and fight them!' she cried, and she *chuk-CHUK*ed her Foby gun.

Chuk-CHUK chuked the Foby guns of the Biscuitrons.

'Wait wait wait!' I said. 'It was my fault! I played the wrong thing, at the wrong time, and . . . this is my fault.'

There was a slight whistley-wind wuff sound as the guns of the Biscuitrons all moved as one to point at me.

Before today nobody had ever pointed a gun at me. Now I had around twenty of them aimed in my direction. I could barely breathe. I scrunched my eyes tightly closed, expecting to hear a **_VAAAAARM_** at any moment. Instead I heard my friend George being amazing.

'Typical Haddie there, taking credit for everything,' said George. 'It wasn't just her fault, it was my fault, too.'

'George, no,' I said.

'Me too, I suppose,' said Naomi, with a shrug. 'So, like . . . yeah?'

George and Naomi had stepped up beside me, into the angry glare of focused attention, a place where neither of them really wanted to be. I had never felt prouder of us. We were a band.

'OK, so it was our fault,' I said. 'We didn't mean to do this. It was a mistake. But we're sorry. And we want to put it right.'

Last time I had apologised and promised to make amends, I had got a hug. This time, I got twenty guns lowering slightly, so they were no longer aimed directly at us. And a hug.

'George, you can let go if you want,' I said.

'No, I'm good,' said George.

'Woah. That's a bold new concept,' said the Chief from inside his hole. 'Apologising? And trying to put things right? I'm thinking maybe that should have been one of our rules.'

'Chief, you're the Chief. You can make it one of your rules,' I said.

'Can I? OK,' said the Chief, climbing out of his hole. 'Um. Hello. You all know me. You know what I do.'

'Nothing?' said Tiffany. 'You do nothing.'

'Exactly! And, er, I'm sorry about that. And I'm going to try and put that right. I do solemnly declare a new rule. Is that how you do it? It sounds right. I do declare that this, ah, situation is all their fault,' he pointed at us, 'but they have apologised and they want to try to put things right, so I hereby state we should, I don't know, maybe let them? Or something. Is that OK?'

KRAKA-DOOOOOOM! agreed the sky, kind of.

'Now, to be fair,' I said, 'this is partially your fault, too.'

'Oh crikey, is it?' he said and he jumped back into his hole.

Man Man stepped between us and the accusing glare of twenty Foby guns.

'Rabbits!' he said. 'People! And Cyril. You know what I've been thinking?' he said. 'Yes, we could have a team-up and yes we could fight together! But instead of fighting *against* something, why can't we fight *for* something? What about that?'

'Ha, sounds good to me,' I said.

Tiffany lowered her Foby gun.

'Biscuitrons, stand down. But, Man Man, I

swear to you, if you don't save the world, we're going to be having words.'

Man Man gave her a wink. 'I promise, whether the world is saved or not, I will fight you,' he said. 'A titanic, pointless fist fight that solves absolutely nothing as the world explodes around us. What do you reckon?'

'Deal,' said Tiffany.

'Everybody, stop what you're doing and get on this bus!'

Of course, just when everything seemed to be going swimmingly, that would be when a Happybus would turn up and ruin everything. I sighed, waiting for the shushing sound of a bus door opening.

HHHHHHHHHHHHHHHS

What was that? It was coming from above us.

I looked up. Floating there was a big red bus, which . . . ah, to be honest, it wasn't that surprising. Why not, eh? A flying bus? It was just one more thing, really. More surprisingly, on its side was written:

'Everything Could Be All Right and Hope is a Wonderful Emotion to Hold in Your Heart But Also You Might Have to Actually Do Something With Your Hands to Truly Effect a Change!'

The bus door was open and Professor Whizz was standing in the doorway.

'Did you like that? I made the bus door make a noise that is the opposite of *Shhhhhhh*. Using science! Because I need you to climb aboard and make some noise. I've been doing a lot of science in the last half hour. I've installed MoodBoard technology on this bus, I've set up a stage for you on the top deck and because I was on a roll I think I also totally invented a brand-new type of biscuit. Ask me about our Jam Bam Biccy Whammers! Or don't, they are only theoretical at this stage and we don't have time. What the heck have you been doing?'

Chapter 27

A-ONE, A-TWO...

KRAKA-DOOOOOOM! went the sky as the bus landed and we rushed onboard.

'Listen,' said Whizz. 'You need to play "Alpaca Waka Waka" again. I went back to my calculations and I worked out why it didn't work when me and Man Man played with you.'

'Was it because you played what I told you to?'

'Um . . . wow, OK, yes. Great sciencing, Haddie. I worked it out by doing some mad equations on the sciPad using quantum chaos theory. How'd you work it out?'

'I think I always knew,' I said. 'When you're in

a band, the important thing is sometimes to do it wrong in exactly the right way. And for that, I need George and Naomi.'

'Well, rock on,' said Whizz. 'Go on, up to the top deck, that's where the gear is. Get yourselves set up. I'll get everybody else on board.'

The barrier blocking off the upper deck had been removed. We climbed the stairs.

'So we're playing "Alpaca Waka Waka",' said George. 'I can't remember how that one goes.'

'You'll know,' I said.

'Well, obviously, you'll tell me.'

'Nah,' I said. 'You'll know. Play what you feel.'

'I feel nervous. Terrified, actually.'

'Play that then. You OK, Naomi?'

We'd got to the top of the stairs. Naomi looked at the makeshift stage Whizz had set up at the back of the bus. She blew a stray bit of fringe from her forehead in the coolest way possible.

'I am very frightened indeed, but if the world is going to end, I'd like to be with you when it does,' she said, with a smile. 'And I'd like to be myself.'

No irony. No attitude. Just sincerity. She is *so cool.*

She took her wig off and shook her gorgeous fluffy ears free.

We clambered on to the stage.

KRAKA-DOOOOOOM!

I pulled El Jirafa from the scabbard on my back and strapped her around my neck.

Naomi had her bass on. George was sat behind the Tupperware, staring at it like he was worried it was going to jump up and bite his face off.

At the other end of the bus the Biscuitrons were trooping up the stairs.

'OK everyone, move towards the stage, carefully now, I'm just going to launch the bus.' Whizz licked his finger and stuck it in the air. 'Oh yes, we are primed for a dandy take-off. The waves of anticipation here are epic!'

'So . . . is there a reason you needed everybody here?' I said. 'Like, something to do with the acoustic properties of the noise we'll make? Or will they act like an amplification of the vibrations? Or—'

'Haha, no,' said the professor. 'Same reason I set this all up on a flying bus. I just thought it would be more fun this way. Not going to lie though, Haddie, we've only got time for one shot at this, so you'd better make sure you get it wrong in the most right way possible on your first try. You ready?' He lifted his sciPad and swiped his fingers across it.

The bus wiggled. It jiggled. It bucked.

WHOOOOOOOOSH

We had lift-off. The bus soared into the orange-crazed sky.

I nodded to my bandmates. George didn't respond. He had turned green. Actually, physically green. Apart from his hair, which was still a sandy colour. He looked autumnal, like a tree whose leaves were about to fall off. Maybe that was symbolic of the way he felt his life was going, I don't know.

238

Naomi just looked cool, standing motionless behind her bass guitar, her long, brown rabbit ears flapping in the wind at just the right angle. Who knows what she was thinking. Probably something with a hashtag in front of it.

I closed my eyes, just to savour the moment.

KRAKA-DOOOOOOM!

'So, not to rush you guys,' said the professor, 'but there's a hole in the sky you could drive a bus through, and I am driving a bus in the sky near that hole, so, you know, you do the maths.'

OK then. It was time to do this.

I looked down at the fret of my guitar.

'C'mon, El Jirafa,' I murmured.

I placed my fingers in the shape of F minus, the most uniquely unique of all the chords I had ever dreamed up.

I looked to my left. There was Naomi, bass slung round her neck, looking as cool as deep space on a chilly morning.

'Ready?' I mouthed.

She nodded.

I turned to look behind me. There was George, sitting behind his Tupperware.

'Ready?' I mouthed.

He shook his head.

'George, you can do this. You don't have to do this. But you can. Do you believe me?'

He nodded.

The top deck of the bus was full. Of humans, of rabbits, of Cyril, all gazing expectantly at us. A crowd of individuals had become an audience, and as one they were waiting anxiously to see what was going to happen next.

Me too.

'OK,' I said and I stepped up to the microphone. 'A-one, a-two . . .'

If you're on a stage and you have an instrument in front of you, and an audience in front of you and your instrument, and you hear the words 'one two three four' it's like you're on a roller coaster, and the carriages have been cranked up to the top of the first drop, and on 'four' the

240

brakes are released and whooooosh – down you go. You just start playing. There's nothing else you can do.

'I can't do this,' I said. And I sat down on the front of the stage and covered my face with my hands in case anyone could see I was crying.

Chapter 28

'Woah no!' said various voices.

I felt the bus bank wildly to the left.

I heard the professor yelling, 'Wave of doubt on the, I dunno, starboard bow? Maybe port. I'd need to google it to be sure. But either way, she's a biggie!'

I felt an arm round my shoulder.

'Are you OK, Hadz?' said George.

'No! This is stupid. We can't do this. What if it doesn't work? What if everybody hates us? What if we suck? I'm sorry, I should never have started this stupid band in the first place.'

'There is every chance this will work,' shouted the professor. 'Well, around 0.75 per cent chance. But that's still more than if you don't try!'

'Haddie, I live my whole life doubting myself. But if I listened to that voice, I'd never leave the house. You're the reason I'm on this bus, Haddie. Thank you,' said George.

The bus banked to the right.

'There is so much doubt sloshing around here,' said Whizz. 'But that's fine! The bus can surf that mood, and so can you. Cos if you don't it'll crash over you and . . . wipeout!'

'I'm feeling a bit sick. Is anyone else feeling a bit sick?' said Cyril. I don't think he was talking to me but my gosh, yes, I did feel sick.

'What were we even thinking?' I said. '"Alpaca Waka Waka". It doesn't even mean anything.'

'Use all the waves that are available to you,' said Whizz. 'The more waves, the harder and faster you'll go.'

'The thing with waves is you can't punch them,' said Man Man. 'Well, you can. I have tried, one time. But it was pointless. The tide still came in.'

'Just be yourself,' said Naomi, her gorgeous pink nose twitching in a truly comforting way.

'It'll be all right,' said George.

Everyone was reassuring me. It felt weird. Normally I was the one doing the reassuring. It was nice.

'You're more believable than a bus, George,' I said.

'Wow. Thanks.'

Heck it, I thought.

If you're going down anyway, you might as well go down singing.

I stood back up. I wiped the tears from my eyes. I felt the waves of doubt and fear and nausea swelling around me.

And I surfed them, all the way back to behind the microphone.

I gave it a tap.

'OK, hello, Normalton! We are . . .'

Oh heck, what was our band name today?

Oh yes, I had a good one.

'We are the Department for Closing Holes in Reality. And this is our first song. A-one, a-two, a-one two three four!'

We started playing.

BATTERCLATTER went George on the Tupperware.

BADOMBUBOMBOM went Naomi on her bass guitar.

SKA-DANNNNNNNNNNG went El Jirafa Tremendo.

'ALPACA WAKA WAKA,' went me, into the microphone.

MOWMOWMOW went the fabric of reality around us. This was a new part of the song, but it's not as if I was going to tell the universe to shut up and play something different, and anyway I liked it.

We kept playing.

A colossal set of double doors shimmered into existence in the sky above our heads. They were perfectly normal doors, apart from the crackles of lime-green energy that snaked and spat around them. And there was an enormous sign sellotaped to them marked 'WAY OUT'.

BATTERCLATTER

went George on the Tupperware.

BADOMBUBOMBOM

went Naomi on her bass guitar.

They were doing it wrong. In exactly the right way.

SKA-DANNNNNNNNNNG

went El Jirafa Tremendo.

'ALPACA WAKA WAKA,'

went me, into the microphone.

The doors wiggled. Jiggled. Bucked. But they did not open.

'We need more . . . something!' shouted Whizz over the racket we were making.

'ALPACA WAKA WAKA,' I sang, and then just before the next bit I shouted, 'Everyone!'

BATTERCLATTER

went George on the Tupperware.

BADOMBUBOMBOM

went Naomi on her bass guitar.

SKA-DANNNNNNNNNNG

went El Jirafa Tremendo.

'ALPACA WAKA WAKA,'

went me and Cyril, from the crowd. He was clapping along, too. I liked Cyril.

BATTERCLATTER

went George on the Tupperware.

BADOMBUBOMBOM

went Naomi on her bass guitar.

SKA-DANNNNNNNNNNG

went El Jirafa Tremendo.

'ALPACA WAKA WAKA,'

went me and Cyril and Man Man and Bethany and Tiffany, from the crowd.

The doors in the sky cracked open.

BATTERCLATTER

went George on the Tupperware.

BADOMBUBOMBOM

went Naomi on her bass guitar.

SKA-DANNNNNNNNNNG

went El Jirafa Tremendo.

'ALPACA WAKA WAKA,'

went me, and everyone on the bus. Everyone was singing 'Alpaca Waka Waka' along with us.

What did 'Alpaca Waka Waka' mean? Right

then, it meant everything.

The doors in the sky swung open with a

WOAH YEAH!

And that's when everything went REALLY weird.

The world changed, just briefly.

Just briefly, there were infinite worlds, infinite possibilities, all superimposed on top of each other. It was like a huge, blurry, 3D picture of everything and nothing and all things in between.

'ALPACA WAKA WAKA,' we sang.

Maybe we had opened a door into all realities. I don't know, I'm not a scientist, I'm a musician.

Kind of.

And then the air around the bus was filled with fuzzy, orange Bumblefluffs floating gently up into the door in the sky. They were translucent. Some passed through the bus as we played. It was a truly magical spectacle, only spoiled a bit by the fact that each one said, 'LATERS TATERS' as they passed. They really were super-irritating, right up till the end.

Gradually the stream of ABCs slowed until there was just one left, hovering above our heads.

It looked down on us and smiled a huge, benevolent, even-toothed smile, and then it burped. Of course it did. And then it too disappeared through the enormous double doors marked WAY OUT, which then shimmered and disappeared with a

Pop!

And that was that, apart from the last two verses of 'Alpaca Waka Waka'.

'ALPACA WAKA WAKA,' we sang.

And then we stopped.

The bus flew on, across a sky that was blue and entirely free of orange crackles.

I looked over at the professor. 'Did we save the world?'

He swiped at his sciPad.

'For now, yes,' he said. 'Yes, the WayDoor has been permanently closed.'

And everyone on the bus cheered and whooped and hugged each other.

'Thank you very much,' I said into the microphone. 'We have been The Department for Closing Holes in Reality. And so have you.'

There was another cheer.

'Shall we do another song?' I asked. 'While we're here?'

The cheering stopped.

'Heck no,' said Man Man.

'Are you kidding? That was without a doubt the worst song I have ever heard,' said Tiffany. 'Thanks for saving the world, though.'

'Oh yes, thanks for that,' said Mrs Fluffywhiskers. 'But if you start playing again I'm going to jump off this bus, I don't care how high we are.'

It was a little deflating but then our music is not for everybody. It's better than that.

'Oof,' I said, because George had launched a flying hug at my midriff. Naomi bundled in.

'Group hug!'

'Excuse me.' It was Cyril. 'Will you be doing any more gigs? I really enjoyed that.'

We had a fan! We'd saved the world and we had a fan! What could be better than that?

I looked out over Normalton from the top deck of the flying bus. People had started to emerge from their houses, going about their normal business. Would they ever know what had happened today? Would they learn from it?

The bus was coming in to land.

I spotted Blankley, standing by the road, pointedly looking at anything but the flying bus I was on.

I shouted down at him: 'Blankley! I'm on a flying bus. We just did a gig and saved the world!'

'I doubt that!' he shouted, his eyes still determinedly avoiding the bus that couldn't possibly be flying.

So now I knew.

Everything really was back to normal.

Chapter 29

WOOOOOOOOOO! (TWO)

Normal

Normal is what everything is again, and it is also what everything was, even yesterday when you might have thought, 'Hmmm not sure this is normal'... well it was! OK? And it always was and it always will be especially now the BIG HECKIN MONSTER THAT WAS SITTING ON THE KEYBOARD HAS GONE! ←----- who wrote this? See me!

[extracted from *Biccypedia*]

It was a lovely Sunday morning and I awoke to the sounds of the summer.

Because it was Sunday morning, I could

hear the groans, grunts and inappropriate *heckity heck*ing of Mum doing nothing in an uncomfortable position downstairs. She calls it 'planking' and she reckons it 'improves her core strength', but so would sticking a scaffolding pole down her neck, and if you ask me that would be less painful and would also increase her intake of iron without the need for eating broccoli, which to me would be a win-win, but what do I know?

I sprang out of bed. Today, I thought, would be a great day for a band practice. And maybe George or Naomi might want to write a song or two, which would be quite exciting, but also that night I had dreamed of a whole new chord, 'G-whizz', which I felt would revolutionise music on this planet for ever, and would hopefully not open any dimensional breaches.

All in all, it was going to be a truly fabooly day, I thought. And then I thought *WOOOOOOOOOOOOOOOOOO!*

Only of course I didn't think that. It was the

shrill, piercing *WOOOOOOO!* of the old air-raid siren on top of Carpenter's Hill.

I rolled my eyes. And if I'm honest, my eyes didn't just roll, they did three kickflips, an ollie and a perfect railslide. That sound was vexing me so much my eyes were doing skateboarding moves.

And then I turned to face you, right out of the page. I looked at you and you looked at me. I waved at you. And I shouldn't be able to do that. Obviously, the walls between realities had weakened again. And as happy as I was to see that you were reading this book and had got all the way to the end – and thank you for that, by the way, I hope you enjoyed it – I couldn't help but ask:

What had those chumps at the Biscuit Factory done *now*?

WOAH YEAH!

hello,
the BISCUIT factory
My name is Trevor
Ask me about our
Nibbly NomNoms!

ACKNOWLEDGEMENTS

THANK YOU TO ALL THE LOVELY PEOPLE AT NEW WRITING NORTH FOR RUNNING THE NORTHERN WRITERS' AWARDS WHICH ARE BRILLIANT (AND I'D SAY THAT EVEN IF I HADN'T WON ONE), AND ESPECIALLY TO WILL MACKIE FOR BEING MINT.

THANK YOU TO HACHETTE FOR SUPPORTING, AND BESTOWING UTTERLY BONKERS PRIZES UPON, NORTHERN WRITERS WITH THEIR CHILDREN'S NOVEL AWARD.

THANK YOU TO TRULY FABOOLY EDITOR RACHEL WADE WHO HELPED THIS BOOK ACTUALLY MAKE SENSE WHILE ALSO MAKING IT MORE BARMY THAN IT WAS TO START WITH.

THANK YOU LAURA DEGNAN. MOST OF THIS IS YOUR FAULT.
I LOVE YOU X

OH, AND THANK *YOU*. YEAH, **YOU**.
YOU KNOW WHO YOU ARE.
AND IF YOU *DON'T* KNOW WHO YOU ARE,
MAYBE CHECK YOUR NAME BADGE?

ABOUT JAMES HARRIS

JAMES HARRIS IS A WRITER, FILMMAKER, PERFORMER, POLE-VAULTER, WIZARD AND EXAGGERATOR BASED IN MIDDLESBROUGH. HE IS A MENTOR AND WORKSHOP LEADER FOR WRITERS' BLOCK NORTH EAST, A TEESSIDE CREATIVE WRITING AND DEVELOPMENT SERVICE.

THE UNBELIEVABLE BISCUIT FACTORY IS HIS FIRST NOVEL, WINNER OF THE NORTHERN WRITERS' CHILDREN'S NOVEL AWARD.

HE'S MADE SHORT FILMS, SKETCHES AND ANIMATIONS FOR THE BBC AND CHANNEL 4, AND HE SOMETIMES PERFORMS LIVE COMEDY WITH HIS FRIENDS.